Rachel

Our CANADIAN *Girl*

Rachel

LYNNE KOSITSKY

PUFFIN
CANADA

PUFFIN CANADA

Published by the Penguin Group

Penguin Group (Canada), 90 Eglinton Avenue East, Suite 700, Toronto, Ontario, Canada M4P 2Y3
(a division of Pearson Canada Inc.)

Penguin Group (USA) Inc., 375 Hudson Street, New York, New York 10014, U.S.A.
Penguin Books Ltd, 80 Strand, London WC2R 0RL, England
Penguin Ireland, 25 St Stephen's Green, Dublin 2, Ireland (a division of Penguin Books Ltd)
Penguin Group (Australia), 250 Camberwell Road, Camberwell, Victoria 3124, Australia
(a division of Pearson Australia Group Pty Ltd)
Penguin Books India Pvt Ltd, 11 Community Centre, Panchsheel Park, New Delhi – 110 017, India
Penguin Group (NZ), 67 Apollo Drive, Rosedale, North Shore 0632, New Zealand
(a division of Pearson New Zealand Ltd)
Penguin Books (South Africa) (Pty) Ltd, 24 Sturdee Avenue, Rosebank,
Johannesburg 2196, South Africa

Penguin Books Ltd, Registered Offices: 80 Strand, London WC2R 0RL, England

First published 2010

1 2 3 4 5 6 7 8 9 10   (WEB)

Design: Matthews Communications Design Inc.
Interior and chapter-opening illustrations (A Mighty Big Imagining, Certificate of Freedom,
An Elephant Tree Christmas) copyright © Ron Lightburn
Interior illustrations (The Maybe House) copyright © Heather Collins
Map and chapter-opening illustrations (The Maybe House) copyright © Sharon Matthews

Manufactured in Canada.

LIBRARY AND ARCHIVES CANADA CATALOGUING IN PUBLICATION

Kositsky, Lynne, 1947-
Rachel / Lynne Kositsky.

(Our Canadian girl)
A compilation of four previously published titles : A mighty
big imagining, 2001; The maybe house, 2002; Certificate
of freedom, 2003; and An elephant tree Christmas, 2004.
ISBN 978-0-14-317084-6

1. Black Canadians—Nova Scotia—Shelbourne—History—18th century—Juvenile fiction. I. Title.
II. Series: Our Canadian girl.

PS8571.O85R32 2010   jC813'.54   C2010-901625-4

Visit the Penguin Group (Canada) website at **www.penguin.ca**

Special and corporate bulk purchase rates available; please see
www.penguin.ca/corporatesales or call 1-800-810-3104, ext. 2477 or 2474

For children everywhere,
in the sincere hope that they will experience
freedom and happiness

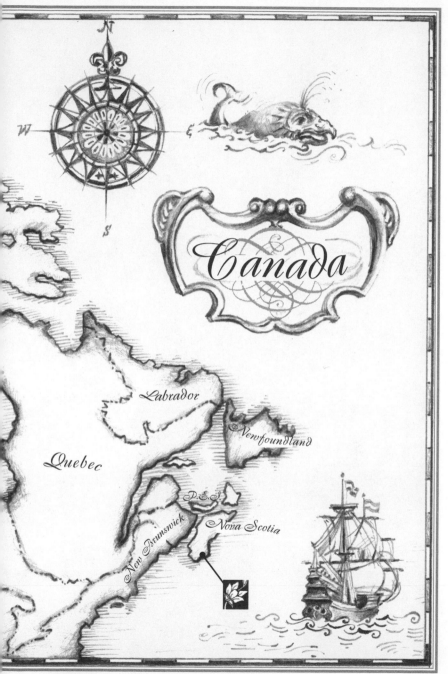

Canada

Labrador

Newfoundland

Quebec

P.E.I.

New Brunswick   Nova Scotia

 Marks the location of the story

MEET RACHEL

I T IS HARD ENOUGH TO IMAGINE LIFE WITHOUT TV, electricity, or running water. Now try to picture living without enough food or clothing, without a comfortable home or medicine. This is the world that Rachel, a slave girl of the eighteenth century, was born into.

Rachel grew up near Charlestown, in South Carolina, where at least two-thirds of the population were slaves. Rachel's grandmother was kidnapped by slave traders and brought over from West Africa, together with many other black people. All were forced to stay in the British colony, living in terrible conditions.

The year our story takes place is 1783, and most of the descendants of these original slaves now work in the rice fields of the plantations, planting and picking the rice known as "Carolina gold." It's a harsh and thankless life, and many die before their time.

In a sense Rachel and her mother were lucky during their years on the plantation. They were house slaves and did not have to work outside in the searing heat. But although the master and mistress were wealthy, with beautiful clothes and sumptuous food, Rachel was dressed in thin rags made of a poor cloth reserved for slaves, and was only ever given rice to eat, the spoiled or broken grains that were not good enough to sell. If she became sick on this diet, she could only get better or die. The master and mistress did not want to spend money on doctors for slaves because they were easily replaced. The mistress was also quick to punish Rachel with a severe beating if she misbehaved.

While Rachel was still a very small child, tension between Britain and her thirteen American colonies grew. The colonists, including Rachel's master, were angry that they were being taxed so heavily, and that Britain had so much control over them. In 1776, after several small clashes, a war called the American Revolution broke out between the colonies and Britain. Almost everybody took sides. Rachel's master supported the Revolution. He was called a Patriot. But some people, the Loyalists, remained loyal to Britain and the English king. They fought on the side of the British army and if caught would often be subjected to the humiliating and dangerous punishment of being covered in hot tar and feathers.

The slaves on Rachel's plantation were caught in the middle. But the British promised them their freedom if they escaped their Patriot owners and fought as Loyalists. Rachel, her mother, and her stepfather decided to run away to the British, and although they did not engage in the fighting, they worked with the soldiers and their wives, setting up camps, cooking, sewing, and washing. When the British lost the war, Rachel's family were afraid that they would be sent back to their owners. The British, however, offered them certificates to show they were free.

By the late fall of 1783, Rachel's stepfather has already been shipped from the port of New York to another British colony, Nova Scotia, while Rachel and her mother wait at the docks, eager to join him.

RUN AWAY from my

plantation, near Charlestown by the Cooper River. Three Negroes, my property, going by the names of Titan, Sukey, and Rachel. All speak good English.

Titan, a pretty tall fellow with two toes missing had on when he went away Negro cloth jacket and britches.

Sukey, a thin woman with a scar on the left forehead, had on Negro cloth dress and loose shoes.

Rachel, a very black young girl, straight limbed, daughter of Sukey, had on Negro cloth skirt, shift, no shoes. Took their blankets with them, and an axe. It is thought they may try to join up with the King's forces.

Whoever delivers the said Negroes, any or all of them, to me, Joshua Roberts, at my plantation, or to the work-house at Charlestown, shall receive Ten Pounds currency reward for the fellow, Five Pounds for the woman, Three Pounds for the girl.

BOOK ONE

A Mighty Big Imagining

CHAPTER N°. 1

"*Boats are bad,*" *Mamma had always said.* "They take you from your own place, where you belong, to a country far, far across the sea where you mus' slave for a cruel white missus and massa." All the more remarkable, then, that Mamma and Rachel were now standing on the deck of a great ship in the New York harbour, wishing to sail away on it.

"Name?" the Englishman in charge demanded of Mamma. Seated at a desk in the middle of the scrubbed deck, he stared at her quizzically before dipping his quill in ink and holding it poised above his book.

Mamma grasped Rachel's wrist so hard her icy fingers left a pale fingerprint bracelet on her daughter's dark skin. It looked as though she were afraid that Rachel, if released, might run away. But Rachel knew better. Mamma, usually so brave and so bossy, was scared as a cat-trapped mouse and grabbing hold of her for comfort. Mamma was terrified of white people.

"Name?" the man repeated, clearly annoyed.

Rachel glanced behind her. There were at least forty more Negroes waiting in line behind them, thinly clothed and almost dancing with cold on the wind-swept deck. This man probably wanted to be through with his accounting of them so he could get to his hot meal and bed.

"Sukey, suh. And this here's my daughter Rachel."

"Sukey what?"

"Don' have no last name, suh," Mamma mumbled, staring down at the tummy bump of her soon-to-be baby. She was still clutching Rachel's wrist for dear life.

"Were you slaves?"

"Yessuh, the both of us, at Massa Roberts' rice plantation near Charlestown."

"You can take his surname, then. I'll put you down as Sukey and Rachel Roberts." He wrote rapidly.

A little brown bird landed on the deck and hopped towards Rachel.

"If you please, suh . . ." murmured Rachel. She could just make out a very large R and very small O on the yellow paper. Although she couldn't read, she knew the shapes of some of the letters. She'd seen the missus write in her journal often enough.

"Yes, what is it?"

"We don't want his name. He never did anything for us. He only whipped us and called us bad Nigras. We don't want any reminders of him at all. If it please you . . ."

"Well?" A tiny teardrop of ink splashed from

the man's waiting pen onto the page.

Rachel glanced at the bird before saying firmly, "Our name is Sparrow. Sukey and Rachel Sparrow."

Mamma sighed in surprise.

"Sparrow be it, then." The man crossed out the R and O and wrote something else in their place. Rachel watched intently. Tossing back his mane of white hair, the man looked at her properly for the first time, as if she were a grown-up. "Your ages?"

"I'm around ten, I'm almost sure. I remember the siege of Charlestown, the terrible noise and fear of it. And Mamma's going on thirty."

"You speak very good English, girl." The man actually smiled, and his face creased like starched linen.

"I was a house slave, suh. I copied the missus, the way she spoke. Then, when we escaped, I copied the soldiers' wives."

"Good for you." A make-believe iron smoothed out his smile, and he went on with his writing.

"Where we goin', suh?" Mamma asked timidly, afraid to interrupt his work.

"To Shelburne, Port Roseway, in Nova Scotia, woman, to a new, free life. Didn't anybody tell you?"

"Oh, yessuh. I jus' wanted to make sure they were right. You see, my husband, Titan, who works for the army, he's on another boat. He's gone before to put up wood houses for the settlers. We wouldn' want to end up someplace else."

"You shall not, I promise you."

"Can we stay on board tonight, suh? We're afraid to go on shore, afraid the massa will find us and drag us back." That was the talk all over town: the slave owners were coming to claim their property now the war was ended. The scar above Mamma's eyebrow seemed to blaze out now, a lick of crimson paint on her brown skin.

"You may. We'll be turning no one away. We sail on the morning tide."

The man waved his hand to dismiss them and gazed at the ocean till his eyes turned the same glass grey as the winter shimmer of water.

"Sukey and Rachel Sparrow, free Nigras in Nova Scotia," Mamma whispered as they climbed below. She'd let go of Rachel at last. "I jus' love the sound of that. Here's your blanket, girl. Gird it round you to stop your shiverin', and never mind the holes."

Rachel nodded. Free Nigras. She didn't even know what that meant. No massa to yell at her, perhaps, and no missus to pull her hair. If she were really lucky, there might even be enough to eat. She thought of all the food on the missus' table in Charlestown and imagined herself stuffing it into her own hungry mouth. That was a mighty big imagining, and she sighed at the effort, pulling her threadbare blanket round her. It was awfully cold up here. She'd never suffered such cold. Even the wild, wet heat of summer on the plantation, with the mosquitoes stinging her skin raw, was better than this. She began the slippery climb down to the ship's hold, hoping the future would be more to her liking than the past.

CHAPTER N.º 2

"When will we be there?" Rachel demanded of Mamma. "Has Titan built a house for us? Will it shelter us from the cold?"

They had left port several days before, escorted by a British warship, but their boat had been becalmed for a long time, swaying and dipping in tiny eddies of water. Rachel had begun to think that she'd never see Nova Scotia. Then the winds had picked up, icy and bitter, and sleet had begun to drive at them in a fierce arc. The sails had filled with gusty air and damp, and the boat had groaned, shaking itself like a giant sea creature. Soon it had begun to move again.

Mamma smiled wanly. She was sick to her stomach from the lurching of the ship and the new baby inside her. "Hush," was all she said. "We'll know when we know, and there ain't no use a-frettin' about it."

"I want to know now. I want this trip to end, and for us to be off the boat."

"Trip is jus' an arm long, you can reach clean across it," declared Mamma in that mysterious way of hers, and there was suddenly no more to be said. No more, that is, until a strange ship was sighted in the distance.

"What's that?" shouted Mamma, her fearful voice flying off into the gale.

"I heard someone say it's a privateer, Mamma, a rebel ship, ready to board us. See how close it comes. At least there's no cargo here that could possibly be worth its while."

"No cargo?" broke in a Negro man who was standing alongside of them. "No cargo, hey?

We're the cargo. It'll take us back south and sell us off as slaves."

Mamma's lips went white as pine ash. Rachel, too, felt the blood wash out of her face. To come so far, only to be dragged back. It was unbearable. But as she cuddled close to Mamma, her chin wobbling, her knees weak as cotton, the British warship protecting them fired one warning shot. Rachel and Mamma jumped back as though hit. The rebel boat came no closer. Instead, it shortened its sails and turned away, facing the wind. Soon, to their relief, they had left it far behind, a speck, then a glint, then nothing on the pale horizon.

Rachel thought she'd never feel entirely safe again.

Two days later they sailed into an eerie fog. It muffled the noise of sea and gulls completely. Every creak and cry of the ship sounded as loud as a pistol crack and set their hearts to hammering again.

When the fog began, ever so slowly, to clear,

land, hilly and densely wooded, lay before them. The tops of the trees were still shawled in mist, which also hung like wispy tassels from branches. The sky was clotted with low cloud. One biggish house, half finished, and a few small huts, mean as slave shacks, freckled the shore. The place looked sulky, miserable. And the warship had vanished, gone on its way.

For a moment Rachel felt really lonely and forlorn. But then she spied Titan waiting with throngs of other Negroes on the lip of the small harbour into which they sailed. Titan was immense, head and shoulders above everyone else. As he came into sight, looming like a great ghost out of the icy gloom, he pulled off his cap and whooped it round in circles to greet them. Mamma squeezed Rachel's hand. She was so thrilled to catch sight of his big familiar face after all these months.

"He's got a new hat . . . an' new trousers too," she cried with delight as he stepped out of the crowd. "This mus' be a rich place and no mistake.

There mus' be more to it than what we're seein'."

"This here's Birchtown," sneered one of the deckhands. "What you see is what you get. Shelburne is just around the bay a piece. A prettier little new-town you'll never clap eyes on. But that's for whites. This here's your getting-off place. The Nigra stop, you might say, with emphasis on the 'stop.' Git your bundles together."

Rachel didn't move. It made no difference where they were. Everybody despised Negroes.

"Understand me, girl?"

"Oh, yessuh."

"Then what you staring at?"

"Nothing, suh." She picked up her bundle and balanced it on her head. It contained her blanket and some worsted stockings given to her on the boat.

"Home," thought Rachel. "Like it or not, this is it. I guess I'd better get used to it."

"Is one of them huts along the shore goin' to be our house?" Mamma asked Titan, after the three of them had greeted one another thoroughly. Rachel had told Titan of their new surname, and Mamma had admired his hat.

"Not exactly," he said, hoisting his family's bundles over his shoulder and drawing Mamma and Rachel away from the crowds.

Titan told them that he'd met every ship for the past three months. He must have been hopeful, thought Rachel, then despairing, of ever seeing his wife and stepdaughter again. But as always, he didn't have much to say. He never used five words when one would do, never used one when he could get by with silence. Rachel remembered with a shock how close-mouthed he was. She would have to learn him all over again.

"Well, where is our house then?" she asked, glancing around. There was no place for a home, surely, not in this mess of forest and great grey boulders.

Titan said nothing, just turned and loped up the nearest hill, his long, badly worn shoes making no mark on the uneven, frosty ground. He couldn't run because of his missing toes, but he sure could walk fast. Mamma and Rachel had a hard time keeping up with him.

Rachel still felt just as dizzy as she'd been on the boat, with the land refusing to stay in place. It wobbled and rose up under her feet, almost tripping her. "I need to get my land legs," she thought. "And I must get shoes."

The soles of her feet were red and peeling, toes burning. She'd never worn footwear, never been given any. In the past her greatest fear had been snakebite as she'd darted to the rice fields carrying messages from the massa to the slave driver. She had had to be quick to spy out that fast, evil coil in the grass. Now, although she refused to voice her complaints aloud, she needed shoes desperately, but for a very different reason. She was afraid her toes were going to freeze, maybe even drop off, and the last thing in the world she wanted was for her feet to look like Titan's. When the family finally reached their new house, she'd put on her new stockings. But not out in this wilderness, with no shoes to protect them. They'd be ruined in no time.

"Here," said Titan at last, dropping the bundles and taking off his hat to scratch his round, curly-haired head. He was standing next to a large pit about three feet deep. A couple of wooden boxes, a mat, a blanket, and some tools were spread untidily below him. A cracked china cup and jug sat on one of the boxes.

Rachel nudged forward till her toes curled

over the edge of the hole. To think Titan had been sleeping in this awful place. It was so small, like an animal's lair, and it reeked of earth, sea . . . and something worse. She sniffed. Mould, maybe. Bones. The smell reminded her of dead things, and she drew back quickly.

"Are you thinkin' of buryin' someone?" asked Mamma, staring into the pit wretchedly. "We can't live there. I ain't goin' to have my bebby there. I'm needin' a cradle for him, not a grave." She went quiet for a moment, then moaned, "Titan, where are your wits? You must've lost 'em when you crossed over the wide ocean." Sitting down on a large white rock, she fished a blanket out of her bundle, wrapped it around her, and began to sway back and forth.

Mamma was right. This hole was just like the one the Negroes dug at night back home to bury their dead in. Cleared of the boxes, it might hold two coffins, three in a pinch, certainly no more. Three. One for each of them. Rachel shuddered at the thought, tried not to cry as the first stinging tears spiked through her lids.

"We got to build up the sides with wood, maybe another two foot, sling a roof over. It'll do us for winter, keep the snow out. In spring the white bosses'll give us our land and we'll build a proper house. Others roundabout are doing the same thing."

This was a long speech for Titan, and he seemed worn out with the effort of pushing it through his teeth. But as he pointed away up the hill, Rachel could see he was right. Dark wisps of smoke spiralled up from what looked like holes in the forest floor. People, perhaps other children, were down underground, a whole village of them, living in the dark. Well, if they could do it, so could she.

"How can I help, Titan?" she asked brightly, swallowing the tears that had run down the back of her nose into her throat. "I'm big and strong as most grown-ups. I can fetch wood. I can hew it if need be. Maybe we can get some kind of a roof up before nightfall."

"Good for you," was his only reply. And for a

fleeting moment he sounded like the white man on the ship who had written down their names.

"Seems a sad thing," Mamma remarked, "that you been here all this time buildin' houses for the white folk, but you ain't had time to build one for yoursel'." She got up and began to unpack the bundles, then bustled around starting to create a home for the three of them.

"That's the way of it, sure enough," said Titan. He slid into the hole to fetch his axe to cut wood with, and Rachel scrambled down too. It was only then that she noticed how he'd lined the earthen sides with ferns and pine branches to try to make things snugger for them.

Much, much later, while gathering moss to chink the spaces in the low wooden walls of their new hut, Rachel would suddenly remember Titan saying something about keeping the snow out. What was snow?

CHAPTER N°. 4

No one was talking in their dark home.
Titan hardly ever spoke anyway. There was little work to be had in the frigid weather, and he spent his time trying to fit his large body more comfortably into their small space. Mamma, dragging herself around and close to birthing the baby, had all but stopped talking too.

"Winter has frozen our tongues too cold to wag," she crabbed when Rachel remarked on how quiet it was. "And don' you go naggin' me, girl. Least you can stan' up in here. I got to walk around with legs or neck bent all the time, and Titan can't stan' up at all. This ain't the house I been wishin' for. This ain't the kinda life I been wishin' for, neither. Free Nigras, indeed."

It was bitterly cold, but Rachel was glad to get out, climbing through the trap door in the sloping roof and sliding down its icy surface to the ground before someone could call her back. She needed to be outside, to be free of her family for a while, even though the glacial weather would drive her back almost immediately. It was so cramped indoors, and any talk was a complaint.

But Mamma was right, she could see that. At least on the plantation they had always been warm, often too warm, with their bellies part full, even if only with yams or broken grains of rice. Here they were freezing every time they stepped out, half frozen when they stepped in, and their stomachs growled day and night like dogs howling at the door. And all they had by way of supplies was some cornmeal with white wriggly worms in it and a bit of what the British called treacle. It was just molasses by another name.

"Not near enough to keep body and soul together," Mamma would grumble, as she cooked the cornmeal over the fire. "Only the worms are gettin' fat. How we s'posed to live out the winter like this?"

Rachel moved clear of the middens near the cabin and took a deep breath of frosty air. Ice and ashes, refreshing after the stink inside. Could it possibly be better to be a slave than a free girl? She was beginning to have worrying, disloyal thoughts.

Snow lay all over the rocky ground, had been there for days, so deep that it caught the weird imprint of her bare foot with its flattish heel and sole. She took another step and admired it, then skipped several times and did an untidy handspring. Her skirt flew up and breath streamed out of her in a white fog.

She'd known right away what snow was as soon as it had begun to drift down in fat, wet flakes. She relished its taste on her tongue and its tingle around her toes. The earth was softer to walk on, and she could draw pictures that stayed until there was a fresh fall. Now she made lacy patterns with her fingernail, took a stick and traced around her feet, then kneeled and wrote over and over the letters that she knew.

"That's an S, and that's a P," she said out loud, trying to spell "Sparrow" the way the captain had spelled it in his book. "I'll have to go inside soon. My feet are like blocks of ice. I can't feel them any more." She stopped for a moment to rub them. "That's a . . . oh dear, I recognize it, but I don't know what it's called. How am I going to learn to read if I don't even know my alphabet? And how am I ever going to be truly free if I can't read?" Rachel had heard another slave say that one time on the plantation, took it to mean that if you could read you could pull yourself up by your bootstraps if you had any, make a better life for yourself.

Something stirred behind a tree, and a faint,

silvery spray cascaded through the branches.

"Who's there?" Rachel called. Her voice sounded strangely high in the snowy woods, where the air was so sharp and clear that nothing seemed quite real.

"Who's there, I say?" Was it an animal or a person?

A slight rustle was quickly followed by a flurry of movement. Rachel was almost sure she saw a long black braid fly out and slap across a trunk. It disappeared in a flash. Afterwards there was only silence and stillness. And a row of small, light footprints among the birches.

"It was a person," sighed Rachel, not sure whether to be pleased or scared. "A child, I think, a girl." There *were* children in Birchtown, other Negro children, but she saw them only rarely. Many were shoeless, like herself, and it was too wintry most of the time for them to venture out.

"But that wasn't a Nigra child," she decided suddenly.

When the words were out, singing in the cold

air, she felt an awful wretchedness, a splash of loneliness. Whoever the child was, Rachel needed her company. But although longing to follow the prints till she found their owner, she realized it would be far too dangerous. Slowly, regretfully, she climbed up the roof to the trap door, slid inside, and dragged her stockings over her numb feet.

By Titan's reckoning, it was now Christmas, give or take a day. He said as much, surprising Mamma and Rachel with the sound of his voice. Then he set eightpence down on one of the boxes, his wages for a recent day's work. Everybody grinned, but a few minutes afterwards, Mamma put down the spoon she was stirring the supper with, leaned her arm against the wall, and groaned.

"Christmas, eh? Well, I think we're jus' about to get a present. Rachel, you better go fetch Nanna Jacklin, that ole bent lady with the scratchy voice. You know where she lives?"

"Yes, Mamma. By the shore, in the hut with three glass windows."

"Tell her to hurry. The bebby's comin', an' I need a woman with me."

Rachel was off and running. The forest was dense with snow, falling so thickly that she could barely see the outlines of trees. She moved rapidly from pine to pine, hugging each as she went, trying to keep her balance in the buffeting wind.

What was that? Her imagination must be playing tricks with her. A shadowy presence seemed to sway and shift, matching her progress step for step. She stopped, digging in her toes. It stopped. She started down the hill again.

Someone ran beside her.

Rachel's heart lunged into her throat. She turned and screamed, her voice hoarse with fear. "Who's there? Tell me at once. You followed me the other day, too."

Nothing. The wind roared.

"Tell me. Show yourself now."

Still nothing.

"If you don't come over *here*," shouted Rachel, trying to sound her bravest, "I'm going to come over *there* and fetch you. Just see if I don't."

There was a slight movement. At first she thought it was a bear, a huge winter bear, emerging from the veil of snow, and she almost died of fright. That would teach her to go yelling at strangers in the forest. But as it came closer she realized that this was a child of about her own age, an Indian girl cloaked in animal skins. The girl had long black hair which, unbraided today, blew out behind her, and she gripped something firmly in her slender hands.

"For you," she murmured in a gentle voice that nonetheless carried across the wind. She held out a pair of bright, soft shoes, high-ankled and beautifully beaded and quilled.

"Micmac moccasins," she whispered. "I wanted

to give them before. I saw how cold you were, but I was too afraid."

Rachel slipped them on, stunned that anyone, never mind a perfect stranger, should give her anything. It was blissful, the way the fur lining comforted her frozen feet.

After admiring the shoes and their perfect fit for several moments, she remembered her manners and looked up to say thank you. The Indian girl had vanished.

CHAPTER N.º 5

Nanna Jacklin brought her grandson Corey with her to the Sparrow hut. A very little boy with filthy feet and hands, he was not above asking a bale of questions while his grandmother helped Mamma through her labour.

"Where you get them boots?" he asked Rachel.

"None of your business." He was far too young to be a playmate to her.

"Why your daddy got two toes missing?"

Titan was creeping around barefoot, trying to be useful.

"He's not my daddy, he's my stepdaddy."

"Where your real daddy, then?" Corey's hair looked as though no one had ever brushed it. It stood out in matted spikes around his head.

"He was sold away from the Roberts' place, where we lived." Rachel replied tersely. She moved as far away from Corey as she could in the cramped pit, but he came after her.

"Why he sold?"

"This is the last answer I'm ever going to give you. D'you understand?"

"Yessum."

"Well, then. Because he was a strong Nigra slave and someone offered the massa an armload of money for him."

"So why your *stepdaddy* got two toes missing?"

"That's it. I told you before. I've no answers left," snapped Rachel, much annoyed.

"Pleasum?"

"Oh, very well. But nothing else, never, ever. The massa cut them off after the first time he ran away. It slowed him up some, but it didn't stop him, else he couldn't have brought us here."

Titan heard and grinned. Then Mamma cried out and put an end to all the talk. Titan went over to her, holding her hand and pushing her hair back from the livid scar on her forehead.

"Bebby here," yelled Nanna Jacklin a few moments later. "A great big boy, jus' like his father, but he got all his toes! Fingers too, ten of 'em, ripplin' like corn in the field." She wrapped him in a bit of torn cloth and handed him to his mother.

"Where you get them shoes?" whispered Mamma hoarsely, heaving herself up on one shoulder.

"From an Indian girl, Mamma. She gave them to me."

"Well, you watch them Indians. They not our kind," she warned before sinking down again. "You need other Nigras to know where you are."

Rachel frowned and snuggled farther into her moccasins. Nanna Jacklin gathered her things and took Corey home.

The new baby had very pale skin, which made Rachel wince because it kept reminding her of the maggots in the cornmeal. But right away, everyone else loved the ugly creature, whose name was Jem. Mamma had decided beforehand she'd call a son that. A daughter, which was what Rachel had been hoping for, would have been Phebe.

"And you will be a bright gem, sure as the sun shines," Titan would say, enveloping the baby in his strong arms. "Maybe a hard diamond when you're grown."

Titan was so proud of his son that he'd taken to talking to him. As for Mamma, instead of her usual bossiness and complaints, there was laughter, and she crooned to the baby as she suckled him. At night she and Titan cuddled up with Jem between them, to keep the little mite warm. Rachel, who still couldn't understand what all the fuss was about, felt especially left out when no one even bothered to cook her a meal or admire her moccasins. She boiled her own corn-meal sullenly, spooning in more than her rightful share of treacle.

"Lookee here, Sukey. He's smiling at me," exclaimed Titan one day with great excitement as the baby displayed his little pink tongue and gums.

"Every grin gum don't mean smile," Mamma replied, smiling herself. "He mus' have the wind."

"Give him to me. I'll burp him." Rachel held her arms out. "I'm trying to love you, baby, I really am. But just look at you." She held Jem close to the fire so she could examine him properly. "Your skin is much too light, not Nigra skin at all, and your eyes are so blue I can see clear through them to midnight. They should be brown, boy."

"A bebby's jus' like cornbread not full-baked." Mamma had an explanation for everything.

"Well, he looks awful. And he sounds even worse," Rachel went on, as the baby began to squall. "Crying all the livelong day and driving me crazy."

"Hush, girl. You were jus' the same. You'll like him well enough when he's grown. He's gonna be a good frien' to you." Taking Jem, Mamma put him to her breast, closing her eyes as he sucked. She seemed to be shutting her daughter out completely.

"I don't need him. I already have a friend." Rachel muttered rebelliously. She was thinking of the Indian girl with the fly-away hair. She'd have to go out and find her. Anything to get away from that baby. They should put him in the rubbish.

CHAPTER N.º 6

She looked everywhere, but it seemed that the Indian girl didn't want to be found. Rachel watched for her footprints in vain, often with Corey trailing along. He seemed to have attached himself to her, and although she did her best to ignore him, he rarely fell back or stopped asking questions.

One morning Rachel went so far afield that she came upon a small town. She had a shawl on that she'd made from a bit of woven cloth, left over when Mamma tore up an old blanket to make wraps for Jem. Drawing it around her tightly, she peeked through the trees at the glint of brooding bay, with its dense cluster of wooden houses and banked-up snow.

"This must be Shelburne," she thought, remembering, with a small shudder, the scornful words of the crewman on the boat. Shelburne was a white town, not like the "Nigra stop" where Rachel lived.

Shelburne, as the man had hinted, looked nothing like Birchtown. The houses were bigger, for a start, some almost as big as the massa's house on the plantation. Many had barns and outhouses, and all but a few appeared to be brand new. In fact, most were so new they seemed barely finished, and others, scattered along long, straight streets, were still timber skeletons. Rachel guessed that they would be completed come spring. Maybe Titan would have a hand in the work and he could collect some more eight-pences.

Despite the shin-deep snow, the place was

thronged with people going about their business. Most of them were white, but Rachel could see two Negroes, one shaking out a mat, the other pulling a heavy load along a snowy street. She felt encouraged to sneak down among them, almost as if their presence made her invisible.

She was still on the outskirts of the town, still among the tall pines, thinking how wonderful it must be to live there, with proper beds and fireplaces, with chimneys and front doors and stores nearby full (as she imagined) of food and fabrics, when a shrill, scathing voice cut in on her thoughts.

"Hey, Nigra. Whose Nigra are you?"

She turned abruptly, almost knocking over a tall, well-dressed white boy.

"I'm nobody's Nigra. I'm free," she said haughtily, drawing herself up to her full height and then adding an inch or two by standing on tiptoe. Pulling her shawl even more tightly around her shoulders, she scrunched down hard on her heels, wheeled around as fast as she could without falling, and began to move away as rapidly as possible.

But he darted by, and a second later he was standing in front of her again, tossing back his light brown hair.

"You'll go when I tell you to, and not before. I said, whose Nigra are you? Answer me properly this time."

Rachel had long understood that there were two ways of saying "Nigra." When Mamma and other Negroes said it, it was soft and open, like part of a lullaby. In some white men's mouths, though, it was harsh, painful, sounding like an insult. This boy, with his careless swagger and sharp, high voice, made it into the nastiest insult of all. He made it sound as though she were an animal.

"I told you, I'm free. I don't have a massa. My stepdaddy joined the British army and we were all released from slavery."

His eyes were ice blue. "Why, you stupid girl. You're one of those filthy urchins from

Birchtown. How dare you come here and flaunt yourself among respectable white people?"

Rachel moved forward again, trying to get past him, but he stuck out his foot in its brass-buckled shoe and tripped her. She went sprawling.

"That'll teach you," he crowed. "I go to school and I know everything. You, on the other hand, you skinny great scarecrow of a Nigra, are ignorant as dirt. Now get out of here."

Rachel would have gone, would have been glad to. That's what she'd been taught all her life: to swallow the taunts and mockery of white people, even if, like now, she was burning with so much anger that she saw red splotches every time she blinked. But as she pushed her wrists down into the spiky crystals of snow to heave herself up and away, she spotted Corey hunched behind a tree. The little monster must have followed her all the way from Birchtown . . . without asking her a single question! No wonder she hadn't realized he was there.

Now, no matter what she'd been taught, no

matter how dangerous it was to answer back, there was no way she was about to act the coward. Even if Corey was a little nobody who crouched shivering in the snow, he reminded her, very uncomfortably, of herself.

She scrambled up and glared directly into the tall boy's face. He might be as stuck up as a lord, he might think he knew everything, but there was one thing he didn't know: he had a thin stream of snot running from his nose to the dent in the middle of his upper lip. As it gathered there in a little pool, glistening and slimy as a snail track, somehow it changed everything. Why, under his fine clothes and his fancy shoes, she thought with a kind of frightened glee, he was just the same as everyone else.

"I'm not stupid and I'm not filthy," she said in a stately voice. "I may be poor but I'm as clever and good as you. Probably cleverer and better, in fact."

The boy was so shocked that for a scant second the wind went out of him, and his shoulders slumped. Rachel used that second to push her advantage. "And I mayn't go to school, but I can read and write anyhow," she said proudly.

"Nigras can't write," he blustered. "It's not allowed. None of our slaves can write."

So his family owned slaves. No wonder he behaved the way he did. And how sad that even in Nova Scotia there were still Negroes who had to obey a massa.

Rachel picked up a stick. The boy smashed it viciously out of her hand.

"I wasn't going to hit you, only show I can write," she remarked sadly. She knelt down in the snow and traced out R for Rachel with her index finger. Then she wrote S, P, A (she still didn't know what that letter was called, though she knew its sound), R, R, O, W. "That's my name," she said. "Rachel Sparrow."

"What a stupid name. This is mine," he said proudly. "Nathan A. Crowley." He picked up the stick he'd struck from her hand and wrote the letters in the snow. Now she knew how to say the A letter.

"What does the A stand for?" she asked.

"Archelaus," he said smugly. "After my grand-father."

He was now writing something else, a long something that was taking him such a deal of time that his tongue protruded with the effort and he panted his foggy breath into the air.

"What does that say?" she asked, trying desperately to commit the snow writing to memory.

"It says: 'Get out of here if you know what's good for you,'" sneered Nathan. "I knew you couldn't read."

"Oh, but I can now." She smiled. "Look." She repeated his words as she traced her finger under what he'd written. "You just taught me how. Thank you, Nathan Archelaus Crowley."

She dodged him and whirled away, laughing. Behind the tree, she could hear little Corey clapping.

CHAPTER N.º 7

Mamma was sick, coughing and moaning, tossing on the two boxes stuck together she called a bed. Titan was so worried that he went to fetch Nanna Jacklin.

"She's worn out with the bebby and the cold and the bad food. I ain't even got my herbs here in this God-forsaken place. I'm sorry, Titan, but there ain't nothin' I can give her." The old woman shook her head and went home.

Mamma wasn't even well enough to feed Jem. The baby cried listlessly until Rachel thought to dip a piece of cloth in treacle and give it to him to suck. But on the second night of Mamma's illness, he started to cough too, a harsh, brittle cough that sounded like dry twigs breaking. At dawn he was still hacking.

For a moment Rachel felt a tiny triumph. "Now you know what it's like to be hungry and miserable, like the rest of us," she thought. Then she felt ashamed, a deep, dark shame that sat in the pit of her belly and wouldn't shift. Jem was really sick, really starving, poor little helpless thing. It was all her fault, she knew it was, for wanting to throw him away.

She made up her mind. "I'm taking him outside, Titan. All the smoke and cinders in here can't be good for his chest."

"Cold air'll make him even sicker," said Titan.

"We have to do something. He'll die if we don't. He hasn't eaten for days, and now this."

Titan barely nodded before turning back to Mamma, who had broken out in a sweat and was trying to throw off her blanket. He was exhausted,

Rachel could see that. He moved slow as a land-locked turtle to push Mamma's covers back over her. The whites of his eyes had turned yellow, and his eyelids sagged at the corners. Rachel felt sorry for him, sorry for them all, including herself. She was frightened, too, that Mamma might never recover. But she had to look after the baby. Mamma would expect her to.

After wrapping Jem in two scraps of blanket, she climbed through the trap door and slid outside with him. The sky was fine and clear, still blue-black down by the water, hazy pink through the pine trees to the east. She sat on a big flat rock and talked to him as he lay in the circle of her arms.

"I'm sorry, baby, I really am. I didn't mean for you to get sick. Now take a few breaths of this good air into your lungs and you'll feel a whole lot better."

Jem coughed.

"You must be feeling pretty bad. You haven't had any milk for a while. Now how would it be if I gave you something to take the edge off your thirst?"

Jem stared up at her with his strange, wise eyes, and Rachel suddenly felt he knew more than Mamma and Titan, more than Nathan Archelaus Crowley, more than anyone in the whole wide world. Perhaps he even knew how much she'd wanted him gone. Babies often looked that way, though. She'd noticed that with the missus' children. But by the time they were two, judging by the way they behaved, they'd forgotten everything.

She needed to try to love Jem, to think of him as a member of her family, no matter how hard it was. She bent forward and scooped up a few small speckles of fresh snow, rolled them together between thumb and forefinger, then thrust the miniature snowball she'd made into the baby's mouth. Jem sucked on it eagerly.

"Here's some more. It's just water, really, but it seems to be doing you a power of good."

She fed him till he wouldn't suck any longer,

then sat quietly with him, watching the red sun thrust its way into the early sky.

"It's not that you've done anything wrong," she whispered at last. "Not really. It's just that you're taking my place with Mamma and Titan. I don't feel as if I belong any more. And they're all I've got. I don't have anyone else to belong *to*."

There was a flicker behind a tree. She wondered whether it might be Corey again, but she was suddenly too exhausted to go find out. Her eyelids were so heavy that she had trouble keeping them open. She began to drift, dream back her old landscape in Charlestown: grey moss dripping like dusty spiderwebs from a giant oak, intense heat, the song-like splash of the Cooper River.

She awoke with a start, half frozen. It was full daylight, and the Indian girl was sitting beside her. The girl had taken Jem into her own lap and was crooning to him in a strange soft language. The baby had his thumb in his mouth. His eyes were shut and he'd stopped coughing.

"Cold air is good for babies' coughs," the girl said gently. "It cleanses their lungs, makes their little bodies healthy again. My family have always known this. You did the right thing."

Rachel rubbed her eyes to make sure she wasn't dreaming. "My mamma is sick too," she confided to the girl. "I'm afraid she'll die. What can we do for her?"

"I'll fetch my aunt. If anyone will know what to do, she will. She's a healer."

Carefully, the girl handed Jem back to Rachel and, turning, sped off through the woods.

CHAPTER N.º 8

Many weeks later, Rachel took Jem outside again. Things were going well. The Indian girl's aunt had arrived right away with a great flourish, a good deal of harrumphing, and a skin bag full of Micmac medicine. She'd stayed till Mamma was on the mend, and now the two women, although still a little wary of each other, were almost friends. Rachel had even heard them laughing together.

Jem was thriving, and Titan was earning a whole shilling every day as a carpenter over in

Shelburne. That meant better meals and warmer clothing. Best of all, Rachel and the Indian girl, Ann-Marie, had become firm friends too.

Ann-Marie had shown Rachel how to chew up tiny bits of food and spit them into Jem's mouth so he wouldn't starve.

"Ugh! I feel like a mother bird feeding my baby a worm," said Rachel, dismayed. But Ann-Marie's trick worked. Jem grew strong, even though Mamma was too sick to nurse him. And as she took care of him, Rachel couldn't help but come to love him. She stroked his little head and sang to him. Sometimes she even thought of him as her baby.

Loving her brother was a precious gift, a gift that Ann-Marie had given her. What could she do for the Indian girl in return? All she had were words, with not too many stories to shape them into. Finally, she decided: she would tell Ann-Marie how they'd all run away from the plantation.

There had been many quilts in the massa's house. Every quilt, with its different pattern meant something important to the slaves. If Mamma was making the missus' bed and hung a certain quilt out of the window to air, it meant "stay away." Another quilt meant "massa fighting mad enough to whup someone." The day the Sparrows left, Mamma had hung out the most important quilt of all. It told Titan to come in from his work early. They were going to escape, run to the British army for protection.

This story led to another—how Mamma had got her scar. How the massa had been beating her when an edge of the lash had whipped round her face, almost taking out an eye. Mamma had vowed then, Rachel told Ann-Marie, that her family would be free some day.

"Lots of Nigras have scars like that, but Mamma was more shamed than most to be beaten. And it was for such a little thing. Taking a piece of bread from his table to give to her small hungry girl at home. That was me," Rachel said with surprise, as if she'd never fully realized it before. "She wanted to give the bread to me.

She told me once, but now she never speaks of it. It's a kind of hurting secret she carries with her."

"I'll never speak of it either," Ann-Marie promised, her dark eyes wide with shock.

For a while Rachel was scared that she had made a mistake in telling her friend. But she had nothing to worry about. In sharing Mamma's secret, the two girls became closer than ever.

Rachel was waiting for Ann-Marie now. She spread a blanket over a dry patch of earth and set Jem down on it. He stared up into the pines and waved his legs and arms in the air.

The trees smelled wonderful, fresh and faintly perfumed. They stole the stink of the pit cabin out of Rachel's nose. The snow was almost gone, slowly disappearing even from the dark places in the forest and the high places on the hills. There was a mildness to the air she hadn't experienced since coming to Birchtown.

"How you spell my name?" It was Corey, of course—Corey with his filthy feet, matted hair, and endless questions. He came whenever Nanna

Jacklin was gone about her business, and he still stuck to Rachel like a burr.

She moved to shoo him away, then changed her mind. She ought to be patient with him. It would be good practice for taking care of Jem as he got older.

"C, O, R—" She wrote the letters in the dirt by the blanket. "I'm not sure of the rest."

"Corey. That my daddy's name, too."

Rachel felt a stinging sorrow. A short time back she'd found out that Corey's daddy and mamma were both dead. They'd been caught escaping from their massa and shot. That's why Corey lived with Nanna Jacklin.

"Listen, Corey, I'm going to find out for you. Everybody should know how to spell their name. In fact, everybody should know how to read and write. I just have to figure how to get all that knowing out of Nathan Crowley's head and into mine. He's easy to fool, and I'll do it. Then I'll be able to teach you everything you need to become a smart, free man." She sat back, very pleased with herself. How difficult could it be?

Baby Jem smiled at her, a proper smile. Mamma had said he wasn't full-baked when he was born, but now he was browning nicely. And his eyes were starting to deepen to a lovely copper. Give him another month and he'd have proper Nigra eyes, just like Rachel's. He really did belong to their family. Mamma was right.

Rachel cooed at the baby. He cooed back.

Tufts of bright-green grass and yellow shoots were pushing out of the earth to gleam in the watery sun. A bird sang somewhere far off. Spring was coming, and Titan had promised them a new house come spring. She wondered idly if it would have glass windows, like Nanna Jacklin's and the rich people's houses in Shelburne. And whether there would be stores nearby, where she could buy herself a new shift and a proper petticoat.

"Why the snow melt?" nagged Corey, impossible as ever. He was digging in the hard earth with a pointed stick and looked dirtier than a chimney sweep.

"Because the weather's warmer, because the sun's out, because spring's coming, because winter's gone, because God is rewarding us, because, oh, I don't know." Rachel was laughing.

Jem, catching her eye, began to laugh too, a deep, throaty gurgle. As his mouth opened, she caught sight of two pearly buds—his first teeth! Whooping with joy, she jumped up, caught Corey by the hand so his stick went sailing into the air, and whirled him round till they were both giddy.

"Hello," called Ann-Marie, coming up the hill in time to watch them spin. "You are having a good time."

"Yes, we are," Rachel shouted. "That's because I've got spring in me today and I'm happy. I'm a free Nigra. A free Nigra in Nova Scotia. I'm going to learn to read and write whole sentences and I'm going to teach Corey how to spell his name."

"Good for you," Ann Marie replied, smiling.

Rachel went to fetch Jem. She lifted him high

so that he could see the tops of the wide-branched apple trees close by the shore.

"This is going to be our home, baby," Rachel resolved. "Here at the Nigra stop in Birchtown. We live here, we'll always live here, and I don't want to see Charlestown, that horrid slave place, ever again. I'll make sure you never see it either."

And she meant what she said, every word of it.

BOOK TWO

The Maybe House

CHAPTER N°. 1

It was hot as hellfire, close as a jail in the tiny pit-cabin, but Mamma, her sleeves rolled up, her fingers deep in the cornmeal pinching out fat wriggly worms, was singing:

Now farewell my massa, my missus, adieu.
More blows nor more stripes will I ne'er take from you.
And if I return to the life that I had
You can put me in chains, cos I surely be mad.

"Amen," exclaimed Titan. It sounded like a sneeze. Baby Jem, who sat on his knee, stared into his father's face with astonishment.

Mamma dropped the mealy worms one by one into the fire. They hissed as the fluid flew out of them and made little crackly explosions. Rachel was hot and tired. She didn't care to think about the worms, Mamma's song, or much else. She only wanted to know when they were going to get out of this awful place, which stank as bad as the midden outside. When they first came Titan had promised them a house, promised he would build it come spring, yet here they still sat, four months later, with their arms too cramped to unfold and their legs tied in knots from trying to take up less space.

"Aren't you boiling hot, Mamma?"

"Not near as boiling as on the plantation, where the air so steamin' and wet the 'squitoes near drowned in it."

"And this place gets smaller every day, I swear," Rachel complained.

"Nonsense, girl. 'Course it don't. You gettin' bigger, that's all." Mamma added water to the pot and set it over the fire. She had enormous stains, like spreading butterfly wings, under her arms, and the scar on her forehead stood out like a warning. Don't be crossin' me, it seemed to say. I taken as much as I can this day, and I ain't listenin' to no child nonsense.

"Are we ever getting a house, Mamma? Is Titan building us one? I know he's busy bringing in the shillings doing the building for white folks in Shelburne, but will there ever be a proper home for *us*?"

"Maybe," said Mamma, wiping her forehead with the back of her arm. Titan, tired out from all his hard work, said nothing.

"When will it happen? Will it happen at all?" Rachel was getting flustered, could feel her little braids sticking out all over her head like porcupine quills. She'd been playing earlier with her Indian friend Ann-Marie and they'd each braided the other's hair. Ann-Marie had two beautiful braids, long and glistening. Rachel envied that soft straight hair almost beyond anything.

"Maybe I say, and maybe I mean. You can't

take no more on your heels than you can kick off with your toes." Mamma always did that, had the last word with some strange, mysterious saying that Rachel couldn't quite catch the corner of.

Why, it's nothing but a maybe house. That's no good, thought Rachel, feeling miserable. Then Mamma spoke up again. "Talking of maybe, Titan, ain't it about time you took yoursel' off to that office and found out all 'bout our land?"

So Mamma was on her side after all!

Titan grunted. He peeled a sock off with one hand while holding on to Jem with the other. A poor ruined foot came into view, two toes missing where the old slave massa had cut them off. Titan rubbed his instep, removed the other sock, and made a ball of both socks together.

Mamma, stirring the pot, kept talking. "I remember when we come here they promised us freedom and a farm. 'Freedom and a farm,' they kep' saying. 'You be free Nigras now.' Where's the farm, I'm wonderin'. Freedom ain't much use without it."

"Can't make head or tail of them papers,"

admitted Titan, dropping the socks by the crate he sat on and scratching his big round head.

"What papers?" asked Mamma.

"The papers they make you sign."

"To see if you good enough to own a farm?"

Titan grunted.

"Take the child with you to the white folk town. She read some. She show you how. She gonna set you straight as a yard of cloth."

"Yes, I will, Titan. I'd love to come. I'll stand in that office and read every word for you, I promise. And when we've signed where we need to, they'll give us our rightful land." Rachel's words sounded brave and bright to her own ears, but privately she wondered if she was up to the task. Spelling her own name wasn't exactly the same as understanding white men's papers. She'd seen some before. Very small print on a very large page. She could hardly make sense of the little squiggly letters.

"We'll see," was all Titan said. Close-mouthed as usual, he left most of his words in the back of his throat. It was easier for him that way. Not so much explaining to do. But it sure was hard for Rachel to know his thinking.

"I'd love a farm." She smiled, imagining it. "A house for us with four windows and a barn full of animals. Goats maybe. Oxen. Cows. I could milk the cows and bring cream in for baby Jem. Crops growing in the fields we could pick and eat ourselves. In the winter the snow would cover everything, and we'd be cozy inside. Remember, Mamma, when we first came, you thought the snow was salt and tried to pick some up to cook with." For a moment she forgot the heat and the worms and the stench of the pit. She was too busy laughing.

"Hey, girl, where you gonna grow crops on this rocky land? Or maybe you aimin' to harvest stones," retorted Mamma, stung, and the conversation, such as it was, rose up with the smoke from the fire and died.

The next day it was pouring rain. Inside, the pit stank of mould and ashes. A rivulet broke through the plank roof onto the fire. The rain must have gathered in a pool till it was too heavy to stay outside, ripping apart the crack that they had left for the smoke to escape through. Steam hissed as water doused the flame, blanketing Mamma and the children in a dirty fog. Was there nowhere dry? Rachel felt damp as a cloth just out of the washing, Jem was crying non-stop, and Mamma was getting more sulky-faced by the minute.

"Where is that Titan? Didn't he promise me he be home after work? Didn't he promise he take the bebby off my hands for a wad of time? You, girl, Rachel, you take that bebby on your knee and bounce him round some."

"Oh, Mamma," groaned Rachel. "He's covered in mud from lying on the floor. And anyhow, I'm so soaked I'll just make him feel more uncomfortable than ever."

Mamma, as usual, just ignored what she didn't

want to hear. It was as if Rachel hadn't spoken at all. "He want food but I ain't got nothin' for him. I ain't eaten near enough to make milk, and been sick too much. My breasts dry as a creek in summer, though the rest of me wet enough. Stick you' finger in his mouth for him to suck. I'll give him cornmeal mush if I ever get this fire goin' again."

Sighing, Rachel took Jem on her knee. He ceased his howling for a moment, then yelled louder. She knew she should love her brother but sometimes it was really hard. Feeling guilty, she wiped away his tears. They appeared again right away, like magic, so she pushed her finger in his little bud of a mouth, like Mamma had told her to. He bit it.

"Ow, you stop that, d'you hear, baby?" she snapped, yanking her finger out. "Don't you ever do that again."

Jem closed his mouth in amazement. Soggy from the rain and mud, he was an enormous and slippery load. Under his weight, Rachel's legs felt thin as sticks, just about ready to snap.

"How is it, Mamma, that this baby goes on getting fatter and fatter, while the rest of us are near dying from hunger?" she complained.

"Tell him a Buh Rabbit story, like I tol' you when you was little," suggested Mamma, as though that would help. "I use to tell you them stories on the plantation all the livelong day, to keep you from makin' a racket while I workin' for the missus."

Rachel wasn't in the mood to tell stories. And her brother was too young to understand them anyway. Instead she changed the subject. "I need to pee. Rain does that to me. But I'll drown if I try to go outside."

"Hold it in, then," Mamma advised.

There was a faint noise above them as the trap door in the roof opened, letting in more rain. "Here you be, Titan, and it ain't a minute too soon," Mamma told him. "I was just 'bout to step out in the downpour an' holler for you."

Titan slid down into the pit-cabin. Wet as an

otter, he looked even more wretched than the rest of them.

"What you been doin' out so late?" asked Mamma.

Titan said nothing. He just found a small space in a corner, folded his long legs and arms into it as though he were a piece of cloth, and shut his eyes.

"Cat got you' tongue?" Mamma was trying, with little success, to get the fire going again. She was short of breath from puffing and blowing on the embers.

One eye opened. "I been to Shelburne after I finished work. I made my mark on lots of papers that the white folk wrote. They say it'll take a deal of time for us to get our land."

Rachel remembered how Titan signed his name, with a tall quavering X like a daddy-long-legs. That wouldn't get them anywhere, she thought with fury. He should have taken her with him, like he promised he would. Or maybe he really hadn't promised. He talked so little it was hard to tell.

"Next time, I want to come with you," she said firmly. "I'll help you, Titan, just see if I don't. I know how to sign your name. T–I–T–A–N. And I can teach you to sign it yourself, so the white people take better notice of us. I can already imagine our four glass windows gleaming in the sun."

"There won't be no next time," growled Titan. "I'm done. Now we'll see."

"There you go again, girl. Imaginin' is for rich folks who don't have nothin' else to do with their time." Mamma had to add her threepence worth, bringing Rachel back to earth with a bump. "Imaginin' be a big conch shell on sand when tide's gone out, full o' empty sea noise. This ain't the way I brung you up, to waste you' time imaginin'."

Rachel looked across at Titan, to see if he had anything else to say about their farm. But he just sat in his corner with his head down as the rain continued to drip in, steam sputtering along the rim of the fire. Maybe he'd even fallen asleep.

Jem opened his mouth and started to howl

again. Rachel's belly growled like a mountain lion. Rachel wanted to talk more, wanted to be sure in her mind that they'd get their land one day. It was the most important thing in the world to her. But with Titan sleeping and Mamma's lips clamped shut, it appeared they'd come to the end of the conversation.

CHAPTER N.º 2

"Buh Rabbit met a giant spider," Rachel told Jem. They were outside, far away from the stink of the midden, lying on earth and grass. Rachel stared up through needled branches, glanced away as her eyes met the sun, shining through the pines. Some of the ground was in deep shadow, the rest in dappled, flickering light, like glints on sea water.

Ann-Marie was lying next to them. She stared up too. "Go on," she urged. "I want to hear this story. The Micmac have their own story of a great spider. I'll tell it to you one day."

73

"What kind spider Buh Rabbit meet?" asked Corey, standing over them with his arms akimbo. He always managed to escape Nanna Jacklin, his grandmother, and come and bother Rachel just when he was least wanted.

"The kind that's big enough to eat you up. Eat up Buh Rabbit, too. Grrr."

"How big Buh Rabbit?" Corey demanded, nothing daunted.

"Ten times smaller than the spider," went on Rachel, who, despite Mamma's warnings, was imagining like mad. "About your size, in fact. Now hush your mouth, sit down if you're staying, and let me get on with my story."

"Where they meet?"

"Shh. I'm concentrating. This tale's never been told before. Where was I?"

Rachel looked sideways for inspiration and spied Titan coming through the trees in the distance. Ann-Marie saw him, too.

"Look," she said. "Here comes your stepfather, walking really fast."

"It's not a bit like him to be back this early. I wonder what he wants," replied Rachel.

Lately Titan had been working every day but church day, and late into the nights, too. He'd been coming home when they were all asleep, and setting off early the next morning without saying a word. There was so much building to be done in Shelburne that he'd been stacking up a mound of shillings for his labour.

Mamma had spent some of his earnings on fish from the harbour, and cranberries. Even the sour little fruit tasted luscious after a winter of cornmeal and nothing much else. Mamma bought the cranberries dried; she bartered for them with a vendor down by the shore. But Rachel couldn't wait to get them fresh in fall, maybe pick them herself, plump scarlet berries like drops of heaven. Maybe she could sweeten them with treacle. She just had to find out where they grew. Perhaps there'd be other kinds of berries, too, as the warm weather went on. Her mouth watered just thinking about it.

"Go on with the story." This, of course, was Corey, bothering her again. He had sat down between Rachel and Ann-Marie and was tugging at Rachel's sleeve.

But as soon as Titan was within shouting distance he called to Rachel, "Get home." Then he turned and veered back towards the pit-cabin.

Rachel stood up in a rush and picked up Jem. Something had to be wrong. Titan would never arrive back from work early, never come after her, unless it was for something very, very important . . . and most likely bad.

"I'll finish the tale of Buh Rabbit and the spider another day, Corey. I promise. Goodbye, Ann-Marie. I'll see you soon." And Rachel was off, hurrying through the trees, anxious to hear whatever it was that Titan had to say to her.

"What day?" Corey yelled after her, but she ignored him the same way Mamma often ignored her. It never did any good to pay Corey too much attention, anyhow. He just grew more bothersome and asked more of his silly questions.

Rachel put him out of her mind and began to run. Soon she was quite breathless from rushing and worrying, but Jem, enjoying the bumpiness of his ride, chortled all the way home.

"Follow me," said Titan, as soon as they got back to the cabin. He wasn't giving anything away, not even with his eyes.

"I got work to do here," grumbled Mamma. She was sitting outside with her back against the woodpile, weaving a basket out of the tall grass that grew round the shore. African basket, she called it, to keep the cornmeal in. Mamma's baskets were tight enough to hold water and were much admired by the neighbours. On the slave plantation she'd been famous for her weaving. She took a deal of pride in it and hated to be interrupted. "Why you ain't sayin' what the problem is, Titan?"

"No problem." Titan had swung around and was already loping towards the east with long strides, his shoes slopping around his thin feet. "Follow me, that's all."

Mamma stood up, groaning and stretching her arms. Titan had already disappeared among a mess of trees and bracken before she got going.

"Lord, what can that man be wanting now?" she crabbed. But she was already trotting along, trying not to trip over roots, breathing hard. Rachel ran behind her. They had to scramble to stay close to Titan, breathlessly discussing what he might want. They passed Jem from one to the other like a sack of rice when he got too heavy, but he didn't seem to mind at all. He just stretched his arms out to whoever wanted him, laughing all the time.

Rachel had never seen her stepfather move so fast, not even when they were escaping slavery on the plantation. Her legs and back were beginning to ache horribly with the effort of keeping up. Pain shot through her heels. Barefoot today because of the heat, she felt the sting of every pebble. Her feet had grown soft from wearing moccasins, a present from Ann-Marie. This morning, feeling the need for sun on her toes, she'd left her shoes at home. She regretted it terribly now. She could have gone a lot faster if only she'd had them on her feet.

She still had no idea where they were going, or whether to hope for or fear what they might see. She glanced around for familiar landmarks, but Titan was leading them on a different route than any she'd ever taken before.

Soon they reached a fork in the woods, and Titan swerved to the left.

"Mamma," Rachel gasped at last, as they rushed along behind him. He wasn't slowing down at all. "I believe we're on our way to the white folks' town. Up side of Shelburne. This is the path, along here by these crooked oaks. And I remember that big grey boulder there, the three-edged one that's shaped like an army man's hat."

"I believe you right, child," said Mamma, who hardly ever left Birchtown.

"You can see most of the town through the trees, if you just look down this hill."

"Sure is big," cried Mamma with a kind of wonder. "Near the biggest town I ever see."

Soon they came to a clearing, and Titan stopped so abruptly that his wife and stepdaughter almost ran into him.

"Look there," he said.

Mamma and Rachel both squinted along his arm to where his long bony finger was pointing. Up ahead was a small group of shacks. Negro women sat outside them, talking, cooking, weaving baskets. A couple of men were sawing wood, their peaked caps set low on their heads. A couple were bickering over a fish head. Children of about Corey's age ran round chasing one another.

Only one house stood by itself. It stared into the late-afternoon sun through its two glass windows, almost creaking with newness. It had a wooden door and shingled roof. But it did look quite forlorn, Rachel thought, with no one sitting outside it or coming or going nearby. It was towards this house that Titan pointed.

"It looks really lonely, like it needs a family," Rachel remarked. She hoped Titan would give her the answer she was longing to hear. She could already imagine sitting in that fine house, eating in it, going to sleep in it with the door shut tight and safe. She needed it to be theirs, needed for them to own it.

Titan stayed quiet. He was breathing hard from the long walk.

She tried again. "Could that be our house, d'you think?"

Titan still said nothing. He could be so maddening.

"Maybe . . ." Mamma now suggested, also unsure but tasting the possibility and looking into Titan's dark eyes for guidance. They twinkled back at her, revealing nothing.

"Maybe it ain't . . . but maybe 'tis, sure enough," said Titan at last, his big round face breaking into a grin. "I been keeping back some pennies and building it in my empty evenings when my work been done, this whole month since." Almost as an afterthought he added: "I got fed up waiting for our two hundred and fifty rightful acres and just went ahead."

"Good thing," approved Mamma, who was beaming, too. "I been fed up all the way to my forehead, too. That pit-cabin 'bout to be the death o' me. A body don't know where to put her feet in there, 'cept maybe out the trap door."

Rachel laughed. She hadn't even seen the house properly yet, but she couldn't remember ever being so happy. A family needs a real house, she thought. It's the glue that binds them together. Now she could start on her new, free life.

Titan took Jem from Mamma and whirled him round. Then he led the way across the clearing. "Here it is, son. Here be the house you're going to grow up in." With a big flourish, he took them all inside, closing the door softly behind them to make it their own place. As Rachel entered, Jem began to cry, but that didn't spoil things a bit. She adored the house already, and she could have sworn that one of the square shining windows winked at her!

CHAPTER N:o 3

It wasn't a big house. It had only one room. But it was still spacious and comfortable, especially after the pit-cabin. It had a proper fireplace and chimney, and in the few weeks they'd lived there Titan had even built chairs and a bed for it, with a crib for Jem. Titan didn't realize that Jem had grown almost big and strong enough to climb out of it!

The house stood close to a creek, making it easy to fetch water. In Birchtown, after the snow had melted, Rachel had carried water from a little pool that met the ocean. When the tide went out, the fresh water remained, and she'd had to make haste to collect it before the tide returned. But the water was dark red, poisonous looking. She never wanted to touch it. Nanna Jacklin, Corey's grandmother, had told her it was harmless. But she'd always shuddered when she poured it out or drank it. She imagined it was blood.

She loved being here so much more. "Our house," she would say, marching back and forth. "Our very own house." She touched the windows, the hearth, the ladder reaching up to a hay-filled loft where she slept, with a kind of awe. It was a maybe house no longer, but a real home built of wooden planks and shingles. She couldn't get over the newness of it, and she even did her chores with a kind of pride. Jem's wailing still bothered her, it was true, but Mamma said he'd get over that quickly enough.

"As soon as he know he have a speakin' voice in that head of his, he be waggin' his tongue mornin' to night, you see. Then you get fed up with the child's blabbin'."

Rachel reckoned that might be the case. Crying or uttering, that baby would make a heap of racket. She was too happy to mind him much, though. Her only real regret was that she now lived even farther away from Ann-Marie. She hadn't seen her Indian friend in ages, and couldn't figure how to get word out to her to tell her where they lived. Rachel had never visited Ann-Marie's camp and wasn't sure where it was. But perhaps they'd find each other and still be able to meet, at least until the deep snow fell, come winter.

"You get out from under my feet, girl," Mamma said one morning. "Ain't gettin' nothin' done with you hoppin' across floorboards and touchin' everythin' like it made of gold."

"Sure, Mamma."

"You swep' the floor?"

Rachel nodded.

"You wash your brother's face? He all smeared

with molasses. The things that bebby get into. He'll be the death of me."

"Yes, Mamma."

Jem was now crawling, using his arms to hoist himself forward. He hadn't figured out what to do with his legs yet, but he was quick enough without them. Life had been much easier when he'd just stayed put.

"Now, don't you forget, you come back later and clean that cod for Titan's supper."

That meant fishing out the worms. Rachel gagged.

"You better get use to them wrigglies, girl. They lot more frighted of you than you be of them. An' worms mean the food jus' fine. They wouldn't be eatin' it else."

"No, Mamma."

Rachel was glad to get out, glad to be free of chores. They'd lost their newness and she wasn't enjoying doing them as much. Besides, in her right hand she held a hot, sticky tuppence that Titan had slipped her a day or so before. He'd said she was a good girl for helping Mamma, and she needed rewarding. A long speech for Titan, so she valued it all the more. Perhaps she could spend the money in the white store about a mile down the way. She'd never ventured inside before, but she'd seen a Negro or two coming out.

That store was mighty fine, she remembered. It was painted blue and had small glass windows in a row over the door. A big sign hung down and blew in the wind. Rachel was itching to get back there.

"This is the day," she told herself firmly. "I'm going to buy me something really good, like the white folks do. Maybe a petticoat. Maybe a pretty pink sash." The tuppence felt like an enormous treasure. She thought she could buy anything she wanted with it.

Though the morning was mild, there was a steamy unrest to it, a feeling of tempers just on the simmer. Rachel glanced around her. There wasn't a single woman or child outside, which set off a warning buzz in her head. Just across the clearing two white men lounged against one of the Negro shacks. Their hair was unkempt, as though it hadn't been brushed in weeks, and their faces were hard. They'd been British soldiers once, she could tell by their dusty red jackets, but now they were probably free to roam the streets. With the war over, most of the soldiers had lost their jobs.

What were they doing here? This was quite a way from the white part of town. Should she go back to the house? She knew Mamma would be none too pleased to see her so soon, not unless she was going to take Jem off her hands and play with him all the livelong day. She didn't think she could face his dribble-mouth and wailing again so soon. And she did have that tuppence to spend, the first real money she'd ever had all to herself. So, keeping her eyes glued to the ground, breathing out and collapsing herself in till she felt small as a field mouse, Rachel tried to slip by the two tall men.

Passing them by, she sighed with relief. But she wasn't safe quite yet.

"Didn't we free you?" one of the men called after her.

She kept going, pretended to herself that he hadn't spoken. Pretended she was Mamma, ignoring anything she didn't want to hear.

"Hey, you, girl, stop. Didn't we free you, release you from the chains of slavery?"

"Yessuh." Turning towards them, her pulse leaping fitfully, she kept her eyes down.

"Didn't we give you everything that was in our power to give?" This was the other fellow, who, she saw with a lightning glance, had yellow hair and a pink, pockmarked face. The two of them were laughing.

"Oh, yessuh." Her voice was almost a whisper. She was afraid to take a breath.

"What does your daddy do to earn his bread?"

"I don't have a daddy. Only a stepdaddy."

The man stopped laughing and roared with frustration. His pockmarks turned a dark, dirty maroon.

Rachel was terrified. "He's a carpenter," she said at last. He helps build houses for people who need them, suh."

The first man hooked her in by the neck of her shift and thrust his face so close to hers she could almost taste the beery bitterness of his breath. "Tell your daddy, tell your daddy from us, that he's taking work away from respectable white folk, men who are starving on the streets. Got that?"

"Yessuh."

"Then don't you forget it, Nigra. We lost the war for *you*." The man shook her, spat into the dirt, and released her so suddenly that she fell. Stumbling up, her fingers and toes trembling, her heart pounding fit to burst, Rachel ran all the way across the clearing and back home. She could feel other people watching her from windows, women and perhaps even men, Negro men who hadn't come to her aid. All those grown folk, she realized with a shudder, were as terrified as she was. That made her feel even worse.

The redcoats were laughing again in the distance. She lunged inside her house but didn't feel safe, even after she slammed the door.

"There you go, trackin' dirt all over my fine clean floor," cried Mamma.

Rachel hugged Mamma so tight the wind went out of her.

"Sail don't carry the ship nowhere without breeze," gasped Mamma. "Don't you go stranglin' the good air out o' me or I be on my sickbed again in no time."

"No, Mamma," Rachel murmured. "Of course not." She didn't want to tell Mamma, didn't want to alarm her by recounting what had happened. But then she began to cry.

CHAPTER N°. 4

Two days later, Ann-Marie came calling.
She'd run into Titan, and he'd told her where
they were living.

"How lovely for you, Rachel," she said. "Your
very own house at last. I wasn't so sure I'd find
you. Titan didn't tell me the way too well."

"Ain't that jus' like him? Titan only got fifty
words to last the day through, so he watch where
he spend 'em," Mamma said. She'd been listening
to their conversation. Her ears just waggled, she
always explained, when other folk were talking.

"How your aunt, girl?" Ann–Marie's aunt had nursed her back to health during their winter in Birchtown.

"She's well, and she misses laughing with you. But it's far from our camp to Shelburne, and she's busy tending to our people."

"I sure miss laughin' with her, too." Mamma sounded wistful, lonely almost. Rachel understood that. She'd been lonely, too, without Ann-Marie.

"I've never been so happy to see anyone," she told her friend now, taking her aside to where Mamma's waggling ears couldn't hear. "I've done my chores. Now you can come to the store with me."

"I'll go along with you, but I'd rather not go inside," Ann-Marie said in her quiet way. "Those people in the white store don't care overmuch for Micmac. Besides, I don't have any money."

"I have tuppence, and I'll be glad to share it with you. We could have a penny each and buy a deal of good things." After what had happened, Rachel was still a little nervous of venturing out on her own. Ann-Marie's company would be a godsend.

On the way, Rachel told her about the horrible incident with the soldiers. It had stayed in her thoughts, coloured her dreams. It was a relief, for a change, to speak to someone other than Mamma, who managed to turn anything around so it seemed like Rachel's own fault. "What you doin' goin' down into the town?" she'd accused, though Rachel had scarcely gotten across the clearing. "You should stick around home, where it's safe."

"Weren't you terribly scared?" Ann-Marie asked, after she'd heard the whole story.

"Terribly. My legs turned to water. I thought they'd never have the strength to carry me back home."

Ann-Marie's eyes were full of concern. For a long while she was silent. When they arrived at the store, Rachel tried again to convince her to come in with her, but Ann-Marie wouldn't budge from the front porch, where she waited in the shadows. Rachel had never seen Ann-Marie look scared before. But then, she'd never been anywhere with her friend except the forest and hills near Birchtown.

"I promise to be quick," she said. There wasn't another Indian on the street.

What an exciting place the store was, full of barrels of salt fish and flour and wrinkly apples. Bolts of fabric, prettier than anything Rachel had ever seen, jostled with fishing tackle and coils of rope. Furs were piled high on the floor, and herbs hung from the ceiling. Many small packets, delicious in their mystery, lined the shelves, and maple sugar candy lay stacked on the counter, almost begging to be eaten. Something was cooking in the back. A cone-shaped mound of sugar sat in the front. Rachel sniffed: sour and sweet, a mix of the familiar and the new. Rachel wished Ann-Marie were in there, experiencing everything with her.

A woman in a striped skirt and shawl stood behind the counter.

"What can I get you today?"

"If you please . . ." Rachel began, not knowing what to ask for. But the storekeeper wasn't talking to her, she realized with disappointment. Two white women had swept in. They were finely dressed, with bonnets and lacy shawls. The storekeeper served them first. They seemed to be able to afford almost everything in the store. Behind them crept a Negro girl of about Rachel's age.

"What would your mistress like this sunny morning, Hannah?" asked the storekeeper. The white women had left, carrying their parcels with them and chattering in high voices. Their English accents sounded a mite strange to Rachel, who was used to the long, sleepy tones of the South stretching like taffy across every day.

"A poun' of nails, six poun' of flour for bakin', and one of those maple sugar apples if you got any left."

"Surely. That'll be for young Mistress Mary, if I'm not mistaken."

"Yessum. She sure do like them apples. The missus say if the chile not careful, her teeth gonna rot out of her head. But that young Missus Mary, she jus' laugh and laugh at her mamma."

Hannah was soon served and gone, and Rachel stepped forward again.

"If you please'um . . ."

"Whose Negro are you?" asked the storekeeper, her voice stern. She wrinkled her nose as though there was a bad smell under it.

Rachel remembered answering that same question once before, remembered saying, "I'm nobody's Nigra, I'm free." That retort had been to a white boy the previous winter. But it had brought a heap of trouble down on her, so now she was more cautious.

"If you please'um, I live up in the Nigra clearing with my mamma and stepdaddy. My stepdaddy gave me tuppence all to myself to spend."

"You a free Nigra?" asked the woman, her eyes narrowing and her voice becoming even more clipped. "You nobody's slave?"

"Yessum. No'um."

"Well, I'll serve you this time, because there's no one in the store, but I don't want you coming in here again and bothering my customers. Understand?"

"Yessum." Rachel could feel the tears spiking behind her lids.

"It's not that I don't like you. It's nothing personal. I just don't like your kind." The storekeeper plonked down two sticks of maple candy. "That's good value for your tuppence. Now slide the money over the counter and git." Scooping up the coin, she turned away and began to tidy the counter, folding up a length of flowered cotton fabric she'd shown to the white women.

Rachel knew she'd been cheated. Her heart trembled within her at the thought of the precious tuppence, which could have bought a deal of fine things but was now lost forever.

"Please'um," she began politely.

"Didn't you hear me the first time? Get out of

here with your Nigra ways. I don't need you dirtying my shop."

It was useless to argue.

Outside, Rachel shared the candy with Ann-Marie, but she was too ashamed to recount what the storekeeper had said and done. Instead she tried to forget it, took to wondering about Hannah instead.

Life was a funny thing. There they were, the two of them, same colour, same height, round-about the same age, too, she figured, but Rachel was free and Hannah was still a slave, beholden to someone else. What was her life like? Was her missus kind or cruel? Where was her mamma? It had been such a long time since Rachel had been a slave. All she remembered was a mountain of shouting and hair pulling. Could that be what Hannah's life was like, too? She certainly hoped not. Hannah looked happy enough, but who could tell? When you were a slave, you weren't really a person. When it came right down to it, you were just a belonging. Like a jug with a handle, you could be picked up and owned by anyone. All your liberty could be poured out of you in one draft.

Rachel shared her thoughts with Ann-Marie.

"Everyone's a person, Rachel. Some are unluckier than others, that's all," Ann-Marie said slowly, sucking on her sugar stick. "One day I'm sure everyone will live free. That will be best."

Rachel reckoned Ann-Marie spoke sense, and she felt a little comforted. But, "When will that day come?" she asked herself as they walked back to the house through the tall pine and spruce trees. She was sure Ann-Marie didn't know the answer to that, either.

CHAPTER N.º 5

Ever since Rachel had seen Hannah in the white folks' store, she kept catching sight of her: pulling wood, carrying a tiny white child, ambling down the road with a bundle on her head. That was often the way of things. Once you knew a person was there, she kind of leapt out at you. She told Mamma about the servant girl.

"She was wearing a good blue skirt, Mamma, and her hair was done up in a bit of red cloth. She was even darker-faced than me. I'm guessing she was just my age."

"I don't want you mixin' with no slaves. We better than they."

That's what all the men and women in the clearing thought, that they were a rung farther up the ladder because they were free. Everyone, it seemed, had to feel better than someone else. It made no sense at all to Rachel, especially as they'd been slaves themselves so recently. There was no point in arguing with Mamma, though. She never listened to anything she didn't want to hear.

But, hanging about the bustling town, it seemed Rachel couldn't avoid the slave girl. One day Hannah dropped a load of washing on Centre Street and stood sobbing miserably in the middle of the road. Rachel ran to help her pick it up, wiping the dirt smears off the pieces of wet clothing as she handed them back.

"The rest of the dust will fly right off when the clothes are dry," she said, to comfort her. Rachel was afraid the girl would come in for a good licking when she got home; she could almost feel the sting of it on her own legs.

"Whose slave are you?" asked Hannah, rubbing her lower back with the palm of her hand as if it ached terribly. "I ain't never seen you before."

"I'm nobody's slave, and I've seen you lots of times. Here's your washing. I just wanted to know. . . if you're treated well." Rachel thought of the whip again and cringed. She'd seen Mamma flogged once for taking bread from the massa's table.

Hannah, piling the washing back inside her basket, stared at Rachel in surprise. Her little sharp nose twitched with what looked like suspicion. "I fine, thank you," she said in a high-and-mighty voice. "I work for the Crowleys. They good massas to me."

"Really?" Rachel asked. She'd never known there were good massas.

Hannah hesitated. "All except young Massa Nathan. He tweak my ears something terrible."

Rachel started at the name. Massa Nathan. Nathan Crowley. Wasn't that the nasty boy who had tripped her up last winter? Who had a haughty attitude and a ribbon of snot running like a snail track from his nostrils to his upper lip? She never wanted to bruise her eyes looking on him again. But still, she admitted to herself, there was something fascinating about him. He could read books, real ones with small print, and Rachel had wanted to get all that knowing out of his head and into hers. She still did. How peculiar that she had seen Hannah around so often, but Hannah's young massa not at all.

"Tell Nathan Crowley," she said, almost fainting at her own daring, "that Rachel Sparrow wants to see him again. Tell him to meet her in the same tangle of forest as last time, any afternoon next week when the sun is halfway down the sky."

"Rachel Sparrow. That you?" asked Hannah, as she picked up her basket to go.

"Yes it is, it surely is, and I'm proud of it."

Hannah's tear-reddened eyes now widened with astonishment, but she said nothing. Rachel wasn't sure whether the girl would tell

Nathan or not. She'd just have to wait and see.

It wasn't until Hannah left that Rachel realized how many white men there were on the streets of Shelburne, all milling around as if they had little to do. Most looked disreputable, skinny and ferocious as wolves in a lean winter. One clicked his teeth at her as she went by, and she hastened away, panting a little as she hurried up the hill.

"Titan," she asked later, "why are so many white men hanging 'bout the town?" It was damply hot in the house, and small brown mealy moths were fluttering around the ceiling in the dark husk of evening.

"No work, I reckon." Titan's face fell into shadow. He closed his eyes, exhausted from his day's labour. Two women were quarrelling far away, their voices melding with the usual cluck of chickens and shouts of young children.

"Too many men, not 'nough work. That sure be a recipe for disaster," said Mamma.

Titan remarked sleepily that he reckoned it was.

CHAPTER N°̣ 6

"So there you are, Nathan Archelaus Crowley."

He had come after all, although Rachel wasn't entirely sure at first. It was another steaming hot day, and the haze made him wobble a little, as if he were a ghost. She moved closer.

"I see you recall my name, you skinny great scarecrow of a Nigra." It was him all right. He was sitting high in the crook of an oak, where he definitely had an advantage over her.

"Well, you must recall mine too, or you wouldn't be here."

"Don't know why I am, unless it's to whup you."

There was a moment's silence as they sized each other up. Sweat glistened along his pale forehead and upper lip. In the distance a woodpecker thrummed away at a tree trunk, and Rachel could hear the tide lapping lazily at the shore.

"What d'you want?" he demanded at last, his face ugly.

"I need a favour," she said quietly. Would she have the courage to tell him what it was?

"Huh." He manoeuvred his way out of the oak, dropped to the ground, and started to stalk away, his back rigid. But as her heart dropped into her moccasins, he suddenly spun around. "What kind of favour, Nigra?"

She swallowed hard. "You're clever. You go to school. You're book-learn'd. I need you to teach me how to read . . . to read properly, not just my name."

"So you admit it then? You can't read. I didn't think so, when I first met you, though you put on quite a show."

"I can't read, it's true," she said sorrowfully. "But I want to most awfully."

"Nigras aren't supposed to read."

"They are so." Boys, and white boys in particular, were horrid, Rachel thought.

"Then say this. Say: 'Nathan Archelaus Crowley, I'm too stupid to know how to read.'" His teeth gleamed like the fangs of an alligator, jaws slung open in the dangerous swamps of the South.

"Nathan Archelaus Crowley, I'm too stupid to know how to read." The last word sounded more like a sob. Rachel felt so degraded, so rundown and poor and dirty, having to say those awful words out loud. But she also felt she'd do most anything to get what she wanted.

"What will you give me in return, Nigra?"

She was so taken aback she had to think fast. "I'll shine your shoes, I'll brush your jacket, I'll wash your clothes, I'll . . ." Her voice trailed away. She had run out of things to offer.

"That's no use. I already have a slave to do all that for me." He tossed his long, light brown hair over his shoulder, his head held so high she could see up his nostrils. Another time she might have giggled, but now the stakes were too high.

"I'll give you my thanks." Her voice, very soft, could scarcely be heard, even by her.

"Huh," he said again. But then, as if curious, "Never known anyone so all fired up to read. Why's it mean so much to you?"

Rachel thought hard. It was important to give the right answer. "Because I can't be truly free unless I can read. And I need to be free more'n anything in this world. And then I want to give others the reading freedom, too."

"No."

"No?"

"No, I will not teach you." His voice was as loud and arrogant as a plantation massa's. He turned to go.

"I'll be waiting for you here, just in case you change your mind," Rachel called out after him. But maybe she was too late. He had vanished.

Rachel went and sat in the same spot in the woods every day when she was finished her chores. She would sit and sit until she almost gave up hope, and her backside ached and her arms and neck would be bitten all over by mosquitoes. One afternoon, when she was just about to leave, cursing herself for ever having been so stupid as to think Nathan Crowley might come back, he suddenly appeared before her, looking high and mighty as ever, but carrying a heavy book, a slate, and some chalk.

"What's the matter with you, Nigra? Never seen a book before?"

"'Course I have."

"Know what the slate's for, do you?"

"'Course I do." She was indignant. "It's for writing words on."

"Well, quit gawping then, and come and learn.

Get on with it and stop dawdling. I haven't got all day."

"Yessuh. No suh."

"Mother would kill me if she saw me passing the time with a Nigra. And no wonder. Just look at the state of you."

"Yessuh."

"But in church they told us to help the poor, and there isn't anyone poorer or shabbier than you, I reckon. So I'm doing my Christian duty, and that's all. Understand?"

"Yessuh."

It didn't matter what Nathan Crowley said, how cruelly his words stung. Rachel's heart felt like a big feather that had lifted off on an eddy of breeze, and she wanted to dance her moccasins into the clouds and laugh out loud. But instead she walked over to him sedately, determined to swallow all his insults and do as she was told. She really couldn't believe he'd made up his mind to teach her, but she wasn't going to give him any excuse, ever, to regret his decision.

Corey had come visiting with his grandmother, Nanna Jacklin. For once his hair was slicked down to his forehead, his clothes were clean. Nanna must have taken the scrubbing brush to him, and not before time.

"The streets full of them soldiers, dirty beasts," she said, bending down and rubbing her swollen, dusty feet.

"We use to be all on the same side," remembered Mamma, "only a year or so back."

Nanna Jacklin groaned. "That was war. They

RACHEL

needed we then. Doesn't bear rememberin'." She collapsed on a stool. "I be gettin' old. Can't hardly reach down to my toes no more. An' I puff jus' walkin' cross the clearin'. Yet we come all the way from Birchtown this day."

Rachel was sitting on the floor with a primer. Mamma had sniffed when Rachel brought it home. But "That white boy's not our kind. You better be careful, girl," was all she'd said.

The primer now sat propped open on a big wooden box. Titan had dragged the box from the pit-cabin, where it had been half of his and Mamma's bed, and the family now used it as a table. It sagged a little in the middle, and Rachel had to watch out for splinters, especially along its raw edges. But it was still better than keeping books on the floor, where Jem could get at them. He was teething and left drool all over everything. And he was pretty much learning how to tear paper.

"Tell rest of Buh Rabbit story," Corey begged Rachel.

She snorted. "Can't you see I'm busy?" As it was, Nanna Jacklin and Mamma were rattling on about the outrageous price of potatoes. We never even eat potatoes, thought Rachel, so I don't know what all the fuss is about. There were also folk quarrelling outside, their voices chopping up the hot July air. Not too unusual, but they were loud as Heaven's trumpet, and she was having a deal of trouble concentrating.

"What you doing?" demanded Corey, biting his finger ends.

"Reading, or at least trying to. That white boy Nathan Crowley is teaching me how. He saved up all his Christian duty to do it. Strange. But stranger things have happened, I guess, in the plan of things."

"What's so strange?"

"A white boy teaching a Nigra girl how to read. That Nathan is a mite kinder than I gave him credit for, though you wouldn't know it from talking to him. When I'm better at reading I'll teach you your alphabet so you can be a gentleman, too. Now hush. Go and clean your nails if you need something to do. How you can bear to put them in your mouth, I don't know. They look like black crescent moons."

She couldn't seem to stem her nastiness. Nathan Crowley had been mean to her, so she was mean to Corey in return. It had become a kind of habit. But the truth was that Nathan had been kinder to her lately. He'd said she was a quick study. He'd said it wasn't as hard as he'd thought it would be to do his Christian duty. And though he'd called her "a skinny great scarecrow of a Nigra" again, just to show who was in charge, he'd said he guessed it wasn't her fault she was so poor and ignorant. He'd even brought her bread and berry jam one day, pulling it sticky and squashed from his pocket and pressing it into her hand. So she really should make an effort to be kinder to Corey, even if he was a real pest and could drive her crazy as a hornet.

"Tell Buh Rabbit story now."

The Buh Rabbit tale had been growing in her

mind, it was true, but it was much too warm just then to be imagining stories. And the quarrel was suddenly sharpening outside. Nanna Jacklin, startled, had hobbled to the door to see what was going on. Then she disappeared through it.

Mamma stood up, smoothing her skirt. "You pay no mind to that racket, girl. You look after them children, you hear me?"

"Yes, Mamma."

Mamma stepped out, too. "Nanna, you wait fo' me. I ain't as quick as I use to be."

Scarcely had she left when a shout, more like an animal snarl, echoed through the clearing. Rachel cringed. She had heard and seen fights before and hated the guttural voices, the angry eyes. There seemed to be arguments all the time now. Negroes against Negroes, Negroes against whites. It was the hot weather and the lack of shillings, Mamma said, driving everyone to rage. But this was the worst yet. That shout was like a battle cry, reminding her of the war just past. Corey's face wrinkled like a dried grape, his mouth sprung open, and she could see he was about to wail.

"Don't bawl," she pleaded. "There's enough noise going on outside without you adding to it."

"Yessum . . . I scared." He grabbed her hand. A few unruly strands of his hair had come unstuck and were sticking straight up. His eyes turned down at the corners and tears squeezed through them. Meanwhile, the yelling swelled like rising dough till it seemed there wasn't a quiet corner left in the world.

Rachel's breath caught in her throat. She felt as though someone was tightening a belt around her chest, a broad leather belt like Titan's. But no matter what, she didn't want Corey to know how afraid she was. It would only make him shriek.

"Don't be scared, please. Listen: the great big spider was enslaving all the small creatures, Buh Rabbit, Buh Mouse, and Buh Squirrel. If they didn't do what he wanted, he would threaten them . . ."

"What with?" Corey's face had taken on a hideous

green pallor. The shouting continued outside.

"With . . ." Rachel tried to think through her own fear. "With his poisonous bite. Hush, now."

"I scared," Corey moaned again.

A horrible tearing noise, followed by a colossal bang like a thunderclap, rattled the house. Jem, who had been asleep in the corner, started to holler, and Rachel glanced at him despairingly before racing to the window. Through the pebbly glass she caught sight of a muddle of people, Negroes and soldiers both, all snarled up with one another, fighting. A man lay on the ground, bloodied and unmoving, and a neighbouring shack was collapsed on all four sides. It was wide and level as a tabletop, and it looked as if an enormous gale had blown by, knocking it over.

Flying to the door, evading Corey's clutching fingers, Rachel shrieked: "Mamma, Mamma, where are you? What's happened?" Charged with watching out for Jem and Corey, she felt panic rising like vomit inside her. She was afraid to stay put, terrified to leave. Suppose this house should suddenly buckle with them inside it? They'd all be killed. She suddenly thought of her neighbours, a man, his wife, their four small children. Had they got out alive, or were they lying under that flattened mess of wood and dirt? Jem started to crawl towards her, crying as he came.

Boom. Slam. With an enormous roar, the house shifted violently to one side before teetering back. The wooden floor shook, the walls fluttered like a heart beating too fast. The baby fell sideways and rolled under a chair. This time Rachel didn't have to look. She knew. Another home was down. Bile flooded her mouth. She pulled Jem out from under, snatched him up, and ran. Their mouths were all open. They were all shrieking. Titan caught her as she fled out the door and half pulled, half carried her and Jem to safer ground, with Corey dragging behind them, gripping tight to the hem of her skirt. Where had Titan come from?

Moments passed. Although wrapped in Titan's arms, she could still feel Corey clinging to her, still hear the screaming that came from her own throat. Another frightful roar. With a shudder she glanced back and saw their own home, their maybe house, crash to the ground as the dust flew up and enveloped it. Her one precious book, she realized with horror, lay buried in the ruins of it. This was the white men's fault—the white soldiers with their shabby red jackets. They were pulling down all the Negro shacks with ships' tackle. They wanted the families out, she knew, because the Negro men worked cheaper, but she'd never thought it would come to this.

Everyone was fighting to stop the soldiers. Mamma was in the middle of the fray and Nanna Jacklin was hitting men over the head with a stick. But now Rachel could see the fragile lines, like puppet strings, extending from the soldiers' wicked hands to the only real home she'd ever known. She wouldn't have thought the thin ropes and metal hooks strong enough to bring down a building so full of love. Turning away, she found herself staring right into Titan's face. He was sobbing. He put her down and ran towards the fighting.

CHAPTER N.º 8

The day fell like a stone into dusk.

Others had gathered to watch. The crowd grew and grew, as if it were some kind of entertainment. Torches burned, illuminating the ruins of the little Negro neighbourhood. Meanwhile all Rachel wanted to do was get out of there. Her primer was well and truly gone, together with all her dreams of learning how to read. Her moccasins were buried somewhere in the mess, too. She knew she'd never find them again, was back to walking barefoot.

All at once, Hannah was there. Like everyone else, she had heard the noise and run to the clearing to see what was going on.

"You goin'?" she asked Rachel. Her mouth in repose was a big O, as though she were permanently shocked.

"I guess." Mamma and Titan had said nothing as yet, were digging through debris to see if there was anything worth saving. Rachel knew there wouldn't be.

"Where?" Hannah asked. She seemed so sad, as if Rachel were her only friend in the world. Yet they hardly knew each other.

"I don't know. Back to Birchtown, I s'pose." The thought of it appalled her. Suddenly the stink of the pit-cabin assailed her nostrils, real as if she were already standing in it.

"I tell young Massa Crowley."

"You'd better. I won't be able to meet him now for lessons. I've lost my book anyhow."

Hannah paused for a moment, as if not sure whether to speak her mind.

"Rachel?"

"Yes?"

"Book learnin' all very well. Freedom all very well . . . fo' white folk." She paused again. "But sometimes fo' our kind it better to be a slave."

"I can't believe that. I won't believe it," whispered Rachel. But for the moment she did.

That night Rachel and her family slept in the forest with Corey and Nanna Jacklin. They were too frightened to stay in Shelburne in case the white men came back, and it was too dark to venture on to Birchtown. Rachel was ashamed and frightened. Her family had actually been run out of town. Titan didn't even light a fire for fear of them being found, though wolves howled into the blackness. Rachel could hear other noises in the wood, leaves rustling and twigs cracking as if animals were creeping up on them. Could the two little families be attacked by wild creatures? That would be just as bad as being killed by soldiers.

She wondered with a kind of dread if anyone *had* been killed. Like as not she'd never find out. A riot, Nanna Jacklin called it. Said she'd seen one before, many years back when she was a girl. Some slaves on her plantation had risen against the massa. Both men and women, Negro folk, had died.

"I never think to see this day," she said sorrowfully. "It like the past closin' in on we again."

There was nothing for supper, nothing to cover themselves with. At the mercy of the forest, they all lay down to sleep.

Corey was lying next to Rachel on the stony ground, sticking close for warmth. He wriggled a bit, turned over and over, and moved even nearer, holding on and digging into her with his sharp, dirty nails.

"You stop that, you hear?"

"Tell end of spider story," he demanded.

"Not now. Hasn't enough happened this day?"

She turned over so her back was to him and closed her eyes. But the images on her lids were violent, bloody, and Corey kept bumping her. So she opened her eyes once more, stared into the blackness. She shifted onto her back. Through the tops of the trees she could see a lone star in the inky sky, appearing and vanishing as the branches swayed back and forth. It seemed to be winking at her. One tiny star, she thought, frail as glass, searching for something, for a home place, maybe, like us.

"Look up at that star," she instructed Corey. "See how it twinkles."

"Star?" He wasn't interested. "Tell end of story."

"Buh Rabbit hated that great spider," she whispered suddenly. The story had grown bigger and it was clear now in her mind. The spider was like her old slave massa, she realized, or the soldiers, ordering the way of things, trapping everyone in its evil web. "Buh Rabbit hated him with a vengeance 'cause the spider had all that power over the poor little creatures and treated them real cruel. They couldn't even move without his say-so, and he'd give them little stinging nips just so they didn't forget who was boss. One day the spider set Buh Rabbit and the other animals to work spinning silk and mending cobwebs for him. Then he went away to have dinner."

"What he have for dinner?"

"Little Nigra boys," Rachel hissed.

"Oh."

"Not really. Just listen and stop interrupting."

She really should be kinder, she thought. Nothing that happened was his fault, and he probably felt even more scared and lonely than she did.

"'Don't forget'," said Spider. "'You better be finished by the time I get back or I'll bite you into tiny ant-sized pieces.'

"But Buh Rabbit had an idea. He told the other animals. They were terribly afraid but they all agreed to help him. Rolling up the spider's web, they climbed, huffing and puffing, to the top of the tree with it."

"What happen then?" asked Corey.

"When Spider came back, they dropped that thick old web on him and rolled him in it so he was all tied up. He couldn't get out at all. Then they hung him from a giant oak tree, so he looked like a skein of southern moss. He yelled and he shrieked, he told them he'd eat them alive, but he couldn't get free.

"'You'll never be in charge of me again,' yelled Buh Rabbit. 'I got the better of you this time, you silly old spider. Just see if you can bite me now.'

"'I'll pay you back,' screamed the spider. 'I'll get you for this, you stupid creature, and then I'll whup and mangle you.'

"'Just you try, Spider. Just you try.' Buh Rabbit waggled his ears at him and stuck his little pink tongue out.

"Of course, this made the spider madder than ever. He tried and he tried, he struggled and he strived, but he couldn't get anywhere near Buh

Rabbit, could never bite him or the others again. All his spidery legs were locked tight to his body forever."

"That be a mighty fine story," called Mamma, from across the way. She must have been listening to every word.

"That the end of it?" Corey, sounding disappointed, yawned and burrowed into Rachel like a little mole.

"I surely hope so," she replied, tired of imagining but a whole lot less scared and a whole lot more satisfied. "Now go to sleep."

CHAPTER N°. 9

It was a drab and misty morning. Fall was wrapped tightly round the day even though it was barely August. Mamma, Rachel, and Titan had walked all the way to Birchtown in the chill fog, parting company with Nanna Jacklin and Corey a short while before. Nanna Jacklin had a real house with two glass windows on the water's edge, where she and Corey lived the whole year round.

Rachel's stomach was aching with hunger, her legs with exhaustion. Now the Sparrows stood in a half circle on the hill, gazing down on their old pit-cabin as though staring into an open grave. Rachel held hands with Titan. Mamma was carrying Jem. At least they were still one, still all together.

The same couldn't be said of the pit-cabin. Its roof was gone, no doubt carried off by some other Negro who needed it, the ferns that had lined it had blown away, and the inside was just a gaping hole. The ground seemed to be laughing at them. Some earth had collapsed in on the pit, making it smaller than ever. It looked perfectly awful and smelled worse. The midden next to it had been rotting all summer and was a magnet for insects. Flies and wasps flew in and out, and Rachel just knew it was full of disgusting white worms, blind as night.

No one said anything, but she knew the pit-cabin was her family's home again. There was nowhere else for them to go.

Rachel's toes curled over the edge of the pit as they'd done eight months ago when she'd first come from New York. She felt the same dread now, the fear of never having anywhere decent to live, the other, bigger fear of dying and being buried down there. She could barely face the thought of another winter. She'd only gotten through it last year by imagining the house they were going to have come spring. Now hope had drained out of her and she felt empty as an unworn hat.

"Titan, what we do now?" moaned Mamma, staring in disbelief at the wretched hole in the ground.

"We start over." Titan's voice was gruff. For once Rachel understood there was no point in him saying anything else. He didn't even have an axe any longer to hew the wood they needed for the roof. They'd lost everything but themselves.

"All them high-and-mighty ideas," Mamma muttered, turning on Rachel. "All that imaginin'. You think it come to anythin' now?"

"I don't know, Mamma." Rachel's heart curled in on itself like a caterpillar.

Mamma's scar was standing out on her forehead like a fresh-cut wound. "What you think now, girl?" she shouted. "You think we ever have another house? A proper house of our own, with a fireplace an' a front door, with tables an' chairs an' beds, like decent folk?" She set Jem down and plonked her backside on a rock with her feet stuck out in front of her.

Rachel was about to answer that she was sure they wouldn't. She'd fathomed the bitterness in Mamma's words, felt just as mad and bewildered as Mamma did.

But now Titan was speaking again, almost as if he'd heard her thoughts. "We've lost everything, but we can find it again. We had a better life in Shelburne and we can find it here."

Rachel was turning towards him when out of the corner of her eye, she caught the glint of a brass shoe buckle. Nathan Crowley had come upon them, was standing some way off behind a dusty tangle of brambles. He looked mighty wary, as though he shouldn't be there and didn't know what to expect. A fresh book in hand, he glanced away from her whenever she stared in his direction to assure herself he was real. His face was white as a bleached rag, and he looked humble. Nathan Archelaus Crowley actually looking humble, now that was something to behold!

No one else had seen him, that was clear enough, and if Mamma or Titan did, Rachel couldn't predict what their reaction might be. They were so angry with white people at the moment, and she couldn't blame them for it, felt the rage boiling up in her, too. But still, somehow his presence was something wonderful, brilliant, unlooked for.

In spite of everything, Nathan Crowley had walked all the way from Shelburne to give her a reading and writing lesson. He must have been dogging their footsteps to find out where she lived, and had come—despite his mother, despite his own misgivings—because she could no longer go to him. He wasn't just doing his Christian duty any longer. This was something new and precious to turn over in her mind, a priceless gift. It was even a kind of promise that there would be something better by and by for all of them, Nigra and white. She inclined her head slightly to show Nathan she saw him there.

"Another house?" she said to Mamma slowly, as though she were thinking of other things. "With an upstairs and six shining windows and a fine front door with four panels and a brass handle to it? Maybe, Mamma. Maybe one day we will have one, at that."

"That's the way of it, sure enough," murmured Titan. He jumped down into the hole and began to bank up some of the earth.

After a moment, to Rachel's surprise, Mamma tucked her feet back in, stood up straight, and hugged her daughter tight. "We better fix up this midden if we aimin' to live here," she said. "But it just for the time bein', mind."

"Just for the time being. Yes, Mamma."

Mamma picked up Jem before he crawled away, her scar fading to white, and for the briefest moment she smiled. It was like the fog clearing, like the sun coming out, like spring returning after the longest winter in the world.

BOOK THREE

*Certificate
of Freedom*

CHAPTER № 1

Rachel's stepdaddy, Titan, was building a new house for the family down by the shore. He'd been doing a deal of work for the most important man in Birchtown, Colonel Blucke, mending and making, and in return the Colonel had lent him some tools for his own private use. Titan had been busy, and Rachel loved to go down and see how the house was growing, like a fat, square August flower blooming out of the earth. It took her mind off other things, like Mamma's uncertain temper and the rotten, musty smell of where they lived now.

141

"You're doing fine, Titan," she said. "It's not as good as our Maybe House, but it's a heap better than the pit-cabin. When d'you reckon it'll be finished?"

"Just one log on another till the job be done," replied Titan, who never talked much.

"By fall, maybe? I'd hate to spend another winter in the pit." She shuddered as she remembered the previous winter. It had been cramped and freezing cold. "I could help," she went on. "I'd love to. I've done all my chores for the day, and my reading practice."

Nathan Crowley, the white boy who'd taught her to read, didn't come to Birchtown often now. It was too dangerous. The place was a buzzing wasp's nest of Negroes angry at the whites who'd thrown them out of Shelburne and whites angry at the Negroes for being in Nova Scotia at all. These white men came from Shelburne every now and then to jeer at the Negro folk and make trouble. It had become a kind of pastime, like going to the fair. There was little enough paid work, so they had scant else to do.

Rachel got down on her knees and held a log steady so Titan could saw it in half. "Thank goodness for trees." She smiled. "They're like enormous people with arms outstretched, aiming to protect us."

"You imaginin' again?" Mamma, baby Jem under her arm, had come down from the pit-cabin. "I jus' taking this child over to Nanna Jacklin's. Then you an' me goin' berry pickin', girl." Mamma pronounced it "*betty* pickin'."

Rachel stood up and slung her hands along her hips. Mamma was always wishing her somewhere else just when she was getting comfortable. In fact, truth be told, Mamma could be the worst kind of nuisance, always arranging Rachel and what she was doing.

She scowled at her mother. "I'm already helping here."

"You comin' with me. I need a mess of fruit and then mebbe I make a pie wi' some kin' of cornmeal crust. Titan love them pies in summer. Ain't that so, Titan?"

Titan flicked away a fly and wiped the sweat off his forehead. He went at the wood some more as though Mamma hadn't spoken, his face carved into downward lines, his lips a tight knot of concentration. The saw was none too sharp and he was having trouble making the first cut. Unwilling to behave for him, the log swung out sideways.

"See? I told you he needs me," said Rachel. She helped Titan rearrange the log.

But Mamma was already marching along the path to Nanna Jacklin's, her shoulders up and huffy, her back straight as a ramrod. "I need you more, girl. Time you listen some. You can't tell the deep of the well by the size of the bucket."

Mamma's sayings often didn't hold any sense at all for Rachel. She made a monster face and stuck her tongue out at Mamma's retreating back. But all the same, Titan was giving her one of his quick, curt nods, meaning she should go, and she knew when she was beaten. She took off after Mamma, her neck clammy, her skirt sticking to her legs in the heat. At least she'd be able to eat some of those berries, grown big on sun and summer. They needn't all be kept for the pie. Even now she could almost savour the explosion of sweet, tart flavour on her tongue.

CHAPTER № 2

It was cooler in the deep summer woods, and Rachel was suddenly glad she'd come. Though they'd eaten dried cranberries whenever they could get them last winter, she and Mamma were in the wrong area for them now. The sour fruit liked boggy land that sucked Rachel's feet down into it, and besides, cranberries hadn't come ripe yet. Rachel's Indian friend Ann-Marie, who knew much about the ways of wild things, had once told her that they needed the first kiss of frost on them. Judging by the weather, that likely wouldn't happen for a while.

Mamma, who couldn't get her tongue around the sound of them either, called them *cranbetties*. "Sure would love some o' them cranbetties," she'd say when they'd had nothing to eat but cornmeal for days. The word was contagious. After a while, everyone in the family called them *cranbetties* and looked forward to eating them again.

Though there were no *cranbetties,* there were *raspbetties* and *blackbetties* scattered through the forest, their dense, leafy bushes intertwined with other vines and plants. Some of the blackberries were still greenish white, unready to pick, and they resisted anyhow, clinging to their brambly branches as if loath to leave home.

Their shape and colour reminded Rachel of the missus's pale thimble on the plantation long, long ago, and she shivered. For a moment she could see the missus's white hand as it moved up and down, up and down, sewing a fine, even seam. Since it was the same hand that had often pulled her hair or slapped her face, it was the last thing she cared to think about. Instead she blotted out the memory by working hard, seeking and picking. The ripe berries fell off as soon as she touched them and dropped into her skirt. Too many went by a side road into her mouth, but she just couldn't resist them.

"Don't you eat all them blackbetties, missy," said Mamma, who must have seen the telltale stains on Rachel's lips and teeth. "They for the pie."

"No, Mamma. Yes, Mamma." Rachel swallowed quickly. Mamma went back to filling her little basket, which she'd made herself in the old African way.

Low, brittle bushes with a special kind of round fruit grew among the rocks under the trees. Rachel bent to pick. The tiny berries, which she'd tasted before, were sweet as honey, and as she dropped them into her skirt they made a greyish stain.

"Don't be pickin' *them*." Mamma drew back, fearful.

"They're fine, Mamma. Ann-Marie told me."

"We ain't pickin' nothin' I never seen before. And besides, they *blue*. No nat'ral food blue. *Blue* for the sky, say the good Lord. Blue for the wide ocean."

Rachel sighed. "They're bluebetties, Mamma. *Blue berries*. They're supposed to be eaten. That's if the squirrels don't get them first."

Mamma looked a mite doubtful. She picked one up, sniffed it, and tasted it with the edge of her tongue. "Bluebetties? They the same colour as Jem's eyes when he new hatched."

"And they're delicious. Eat one."

A slight sound, a *crunch,* behind the trees—a bird maybe, or one of those ornery squirrels. But the air seemed suddenly darker, the lacy patches of sunlight gone. As Rachel turned towards the noise she caught a quick flash of red. It wasn't a cardinal or robin, or any sort of small creature. Too big. Too heavy. Twigs cracked. She started, and as she grabbed Mamma's elbow, a few berries tumbled from her skirt.

"Clumsy girl," grumbled Mamma. "All 'em ripe betties, gone for nothin'."

"No, not for nothing. Mamma, there's someone in the woods here. I'm sure of it."

"There you go, always imaginin'. What a chore it is to have an imaginin' child." But now Mamma caught sight of something too, a way off behind a tree, a large something. Could have been a bear, except for the colour.

"It looks like a soldier's jacket," whispered Rachel. "A redcoat."

"We goin' home," Mamma said firmly, the small scar on her forehead blazing. Rachel was terrified when Mamma's scar stood out like a careless lick of crimson paint. It was akin to the weather vane on Colonel Blucke's roof spinning round and round—told of bad storms coming. A knot of hair fell forward, covering Mamma's forehead.

They were scurrying through the woods now, towards the Birchtown settlement, as fast as their bare feet would cover the stony earth. Berries cascaded from Rachel's skirt. They were spilling from Mamma's basket, too, which she carried on her head. But neither Rachel nor Mamma cared a whit. White men were dangerous. They had pulled down the Maybe House in Shelburne with ship's tackle. They had bothered the Nigra folk of Birchtown time and time again, cat-calling, messing in their business, pitching stones.

The only white person that Rachel had any trust in was Nathan Crowley, and he was just a boy. Still, she wished he were with them now. If nothing else, he could make fearsome faces. When he pulled down the corners of his eyes and stuck fingers up both nostrils, he could frighten the local dogs away. She wasn't sure if he could frighten actual people.

"Stop." A man stepped in front of them, holding up his hand. How he'd got there before them was anyone's guess. He must have moved fast, fast, through the trees and run down the hill on the other side. His ginger moustache bristled. His yellow hair and pink, pockmarked face glimmered in the dusky light. Rachel was sure she'd seen him before, but her heart was beating so fast she couldn't remember where, couldn't recall anything, in fact, not even her own name.

"Nigras, good afternoon," he said, kindly enough. "I'm here in the King's employment."

That made Rachel even more frightened, for he didn't look as though he could possibly be in the King's employment, or anyone else's. His red jacket was filthy and threadbare, his boots scuffed and muddy. He hadn't seen the inside of an army barracks for months, was clear as water one of the many de-listed soldiers scavenging around the area. Besides, what would the King, way over in a foreign country and sitting in his palace eating pudding with cream, want with two shabby Nigra folk? Rachel couldn't imagine.

"What you wantin', suh?" asked Mamma, polite as she knew how to be. It made no sense being rude to white folk, especially when they carried long, sharp-nosed guns tucked into their waistbands. They could crush you fast as spit at you. Whisking her basket down and setting it on the grass before her, brushing her hair back off her scar, Mamma stood, arms folded, waiting.

"His Majesty has charged me to examine the Nigras hereabout, make sure they're all truly free."

"Oh, we free, sir. We truly free. We been put down in the book of Nigras, and we got our ce'ticates to prove it." Mamma couldn't say *certificates,* still had the sounds of Africa in her mouth.

"Certificates of freedom?"

"Yessuh," nodded Mamma, her bottom lip catching between her teeth.

Rachel thought hard. At first she couldn't recall the certificates of freedom. What were they? Where had they come from? Who had given them to her and Mamma? It was all lost in the fearful fog of the past.

"We given 'em in New York, before we get on the ship," Mamma went on, as if reading Rachel's thoughts. "Them white men ask us, did we help the army of King George? And we say yessuh.

Then they say, 'You free. We take care of you. You never need go back be slaves.'"

All at once, Rachel remembered. It had been a dark little room near the wharf in New York, with cracked walls and spiderwebs, smelling of mould and salt. An important-looking soldier with shiny buttons was sitting at a packing case for a desk, filling in names on sheets of printed paper. Some people, like her and Mamma, were lucky. They got the precious certificates and hugged them close as treasure maps. But a few were refused. One young girl lunged behind the desk of the gold-button soldier, throwing her arms like tangled ropes around his knees. She begged and cried, she banged her head against the floor, but it made no difference. Her massa was waiting outside, ready to carry her back to the plantation. There she was in a trice, all her freedom poured out of her, a slave again. Rachel blinked as though smacked. Where was that girl now? What had happened to her?

"I need to see those certificates," the man with the ginger moustache declared, bringing her back to the present. "King George needs the proof that you're truly free, d'you see?"

"Yessuh," Mamma murmured. A grasshopper skimmed out of a bush and landed on the man's boot.

"Well, where are they? I got better things to do than stand around passing the time of day with you lazy Nigras. The King's business is mighty important." With the heel of his other boot he squashed the grasshopper. It left a nasty brown smear on his instep.

There is something in his voice, Rachel thought, *something ugly and familiar.* But she still couldn't remember where she'd seen him before. Trembling, she stared down at her bare feet, which were dusty and calloused, before glancing at Mamma again. She was praying Mamma had the certificates with her. She could show them to the man, he would go away, and, apart from a few spilled berries, all would be right again.

"They in my skirt. I sew 'em ce'ticates tight in my skirt to keep 'em safe." Mamma started picking at her hem with her berry-stained fingers, but the white stitches were stout and resisted pulling. The man took a fast step towards her and pulled out a knife. Rachel gasped. Tears spattered down Mamma's face like raindrops.

"Steady," he grinned. "I'm just going to slit those stitches." As he slid the knife along the dark edge of Mamma's skirt, a small bundle of folded papers, dirty and tattered, fell out. Locked inside her hem for almost a year, they'd been dipped in rain, snow, dust, and mud, as her long skirt had trailed across the landscape.

"What's the names on these here certificates?" he demanded, without trying to decipher them. "They're faded."

"Rachel and Sukey," whispered Rachel, realizing with a shock that he couldn't read.

"Rachel and Sukey, eh? That you? And you?"

"Yessuh," they replied in unison.

"These look to be in order, but I must show

them to my officer. Come along with me. Forget the basket," he growled as Mamma bent to pick it up. "There'll be plenty of time for that later."

He gave Mamma a sharp nudge, but she managed to keep her balance. Throwing her arm around Rachel, she gave her a tight hug, and they began, all three of them, to trudge along the twilight path towards Shelburne.

With a flick of his hand, the man crammed the certificates into the pouch that served as the back pocket of his britches. Or at least Rachel thought he did. His fingers moved so slickly, and dusk was falling so fast, she couldn't be sure.

CHAPTER N° 3

A big bubble was rising in Rachel's throat, a sour bubble of fear. It came up from her supperless stomach, almost choking her.

The man had marched them straight past Shelburne, that white folks town, where you might expect his commanding officer to be. "Not here, not here," he chided them when they tried to slow down. "It's a ways further on."

Now they were trekking through unfamiliar country, as the darkest shades of evening began to lower across the land. It was a moonless night with just the faintest flicker of stars. Scissor-like twigs sprang out of nowhere to catch them in the face. Brambles pinched and scratched their legs. But worst of all, they could hear the beasts howling eerily in the forest. *Wolves and bears,* thought Rachel with terror, *maybe a lynx.* This was *their* place, animal town. They didn't need a survey map, like human folk, to tell them where to live. They went wherever they wanted. They ate what they could kill. It just didn't do to be out after dark, and for the first time Rachel prayed that the white man knew how to use his gun.

Mamma was moaning, "I need to get back to my Jem. I can't be travellin' the wild woods all night. My bebby needs feedin'."

"Not long now. Stop yer crabbing."

Mamma and Rachel were stumbling along, exhausted and frightened. *This was almost as bad as the war,* thought Rachel, *when you never knew who was going to come out from behind the bushes and aim a gun at you, and you never knew what side folk were on when you came face to face with them. Friend or foe?* she wanted to yell at the man.

Friend or foe? But when he came close she could smell the liquor and sharp, angry sweat on him, so she figured she already knew.

A house loomed out of the blackness. Just one candle glimmered in a window, throwing a puddle of dim light into the gloom.

"This is the first place we need to stop," said the man, though it was a strange time to go calling.

"Firs' place?" asked Mamma. "How many we need to show our ce'ticates to 'fore we can go home?"

He didn't answer her.

Now the beginnings of remembering were stirring in Rachel's brain. Her last meeting with this man had been something to do with tuppence, with spending money that Titan had given her, and that meeting had been very nasty indeed. Suddenly, the memory emerged, wormy and disgusting, like a fat white maggot crawling out of a barrel of flour. She tried to lose the recollection again out of sheer fright, push it back into her brain, but it wouldn't go. It was too horribly clear, like an ancestor portrait hanging on one of the missus's walls in South Carolina.

The soldier standing in front of her was one of the two men who'd stopped her on her way to the white people store in summer. *Oh, no,* she thought.

"Tell your daddy," he'd said after quizzing her that day, "tell your daddy from us that he's taking work away from respectable white folk, men who are starving on the streets. Got that?"

"Yessuh," she'd whimpered.

"Then don't you forget it, Nigra. We lost the war for *you.*" He'd shaken her till she fell. Stumbling up, she'd run home as fast as her legs would carry her.

She wished she could dash home now. She wished she could signal Mamma, tell her what was wrong so they could both get going, but the man had his eyes on them every single second. And there was still that pistol in his waistband. What did he want with them? Why were they here? It was nothing to do with certificates, she was sure as sugar of that.

"Ho there, George," cried the man, knocking on the door of the house but still glaring at Rachel and Mamma. "Come down now."

"Go away," came a voice from inside. "It's the middle of the night. Respectable folk are all at home abed ... like I was till you came a-bothering me."

"George, it's your own dear brother, Serjeant Gyssop. And I've something special to show 'ee."

Rachel and Mamma clung together. Rachel thought she never wanted to catch sight of George Gyssop, he had such a wretched, gruff voice, and one nasty man, the one they had in front of them, was just about enough for anybody. In any case, there was silence. The door stayed firmly shut.

"What all this got to do with ce'ticates?" asked Mamma, her voice as thin as whey.

Serjeant Gyssop, the fellow in the red coat they'd been trudging through the night with, ignored her. "Come on, George," he cried. "You won't be sorry for it, I promise."

Silence again. Then the rattle of a doorknob. The squeak of a latch going up. A creak as the door opened. Someone peered through it, a nightcap on, with a few sparse red hairs sticking out around it. George Gyssop blinked into the darkness.

"What's all this? What's all this, hey? Serjeant, you'll be the death of me."

"See these here? Two fine Nigra slaves. And one of 'em's for 'ee."

Rachel gasped.

"We ain't slaves!" shouted Mamma. "We free Nigras. You got our ce'ticates in you back pocket, you divil."

Serjeant Gyssop bared his teeth and shook his fist at her. Mamma shut up fast.

"Don't know what she's talking about, George. I got these two off a slave trader down south a ways in one of the lost colonies. I'm aiming to give you the older one in settlement of my debts. A stout wench she is, too."

"Well . . ." mused George, "I was wanting help. And you do owe me a king's ransom, Serjeant, it's true." He paused a moment. "And I'll never see any penny of ought you owe me if I'm any judge of character. You're just like our daddy. Can't keep a shilling to your name. So I might as well take the older wench. What d'you aim to do with the younger?"

"Never you mind, brother. I got a place for her further along the road a ways."

Both Rachel and Mamma were sobbing now. Rachel couldn't believe the trap they'd tumbled into. And to be separated from Mamma. How could she bear it?

"Look in your brother's pouch, Massa Gyssop," she cried through her tears. "Our certificates of freedom are there. We're free Nigras, freed by General Birch himself for helping in the war. We're nobody's slaves."

Serjeant smiled. Casually he untied the pouch and shook the contents onto the ground. Out fell three pennies, a brass button, and a greening crust of bread.

"They were there, they *were!*" Rachel yelled. "He's done away with them somehow."

"He jus' throw them on the earth for the wild beasts to tear 'part," howled Mamma.

"You know how it is with Nigras," Serjeant muttered to his brother. "They'll try anything to tie knots in the truth. These here are slaves, fresh from the fields. I got them fair and square."

"And how was that, Serjeant? You with no money to speak of?"

"I won them in a card game, deuces wild."

"And they say no good can come of gambling. Ha!" George Gyssop stood outside his door pondering as the dawn birds began to sing and the sky patched pink in the east. He stared up and down the woodland path a few times, as if to make sure no one was coming, then grinned, wide and deep, showing a row of blackened teeth.

"Right you are, Serjeant," he said, winking. "I'll take your word for it. Give me the woman. She looks like she might do a decent day's work when she stops snivelling."

"You won't regret it, George. And now we're quits."

The two men pulled Rachel and Mamma, who were holding fast to each other, apart. Last thing Rachel saw through her rainy eyes was Mamma being dragged inside the house.

"No, no," Mamma wailed, her voice cracked as an old crow's. "My Rachel. My bebby. My Titan. You ain't goin' to take me 'way from them. You can't!" As she disappeared, the door closed with a bang. The latch thumped down. The brass door-knob turned.

Then Serjeant Gyssop picked up the pennies and the button and stuffed them in his pouch. Kicking the bread into the grass, he pulled his gun from his waistband, trained it on Rachel, and told her to get moving.

CHAPTER Nº 4

They went around and around, up and down, off the path and back onto it. Rachel was sure Serjeant Gyssop was trying to confuse her so she wouldn't know where Mamma was. And she was mighty confused. The sun, after its first shell-pink patchiness, had totally hidden its face, so she couldn't even tell which way they were headed. Though Mamma had a strong sense of direction, she had none. It was still early, the day unripe and misty, and they met not a soul on their travels.

Finally they reached the outskirts of a small town. It looked unfamiliar, but could it be

Shelburne, come upon from the other side? Rachel hadn't a clue. All she knew was that it had started to rain a good half hour back, and she was soaked to the skin. Her bare feet were freezing, and bleeding from the many sharp pebbles along the way.

At last, when she was so tired and sore she thought she'd fall down if she tried to go another step, Serjeant stopped in front of a big, fine house, two-storey, with a chimney on its slanted roof. It was painted blue, with a vegetable garden out front and a large barn alongside it.

For all Rachel knew, the blue house could have been Titan's handiwork, one of the places he'd earned his shillings. It calmed her to think of him knocking the nails into the wood, his tall, silent figure moving along the logs, planks, and shingles, his big hands hanging loose till it was time to level off another plank or pummel in the next nail. She stood, sadly hushed, her head drooping, thinking on Titan and trying to soothe herself as the rain streamed off her small, sodden braids and down her cheeks.

Serjeant knocked. There was a rustling within, the sound of people getting ready, and then a man, stern and heavy-set, opened the door.

"I have the slave you asked me to procure for you, Jeremiah Pritchard," Serjeant said without preamble, dragging Rachel in front of him.

"I'm not a slave," exclaimed Rachel. "I'm a free—" Serjeant pinched her arm hard and pushed the cold nose of his gun between her shoulder blades, where the other man couldn't see it.

"That?" Jeremiah managed to look both haughty and doubtful at the same time. "That's the slave you have for me? She's no but a girl."

"Aye, but a fine girl, a strong wench, who'll do your bidding. Brought up in a genteel family, well acquainted with all kinds of housework, definitely of good character. Nothing wrong with her that a bout of hard work won't fix." Serjeant sounded like he was reading off one of the old slave posters. "I bought her off Jonathan Slaggs, Esquire, of Halifax Town. Not because he had no further use for her, you understand, but because he was selling up and journeying to England. She's a slave, fair and square, comes from down south, as you'll hear for yourself if she ever says another word to you."

Although Jeremiah Pritchard didn't reply, Serjeant must have reckoned he'd said enough in the selling way of things, because he kept his mouth clamped while Pritchard clasped his hands together and stood staring at the bare patches of grass out front of the house. Now and then, just to show he was still interested, that he wasn't about to go back in and slam the door, he drew his boot through the mounds of dust, making a wavy pattern. A moment later he'd knock the dust off his boot with a hard stamp. It made Rachel jump the first time he did it.

There were heaps of words that Rachel wanted to say to Jeremiah Pritchard, all of them nasty, or at least pleading, but although Serjeant had withdrawn his gun to hide it from his buyer, she didn't quite dare. Instead she stored them in her brain for later.

Jeremiah harrumphed. Then he coughed. Then he examined her closely, as if she were a mare and he were a horse trader. He squeezed her arms, stared into her eyes, even opened her mouth to count her teeth. She wanted to bite his fingers off, almost died of shame when he touched her. Still, though she loathed him already and was all but certain he could feel the waves of poisonous hatred crashing out of her, he seemed well satisfied.

"Well, they do make the best slaves, the young'uns off those southern plantations. They certainly know how to work their keep. This one's for my wife, so it'll be pleasing if her manners are pretty. What do you want for her? Mind ye, mind ye, watch what you ask. I'm no made of money."

"I was thinking of thirty pounds," suggested Serjeant, fingering his moustache. He sounded uncertain. Even Rachel knew he wouldn't get it.

"Thirty pounds? Are you out of your mind, man?"

"She'd fetch three hundred at New Providence."

"This is no New Providence, as you well know. Listen, I've had a good growing year for potatoes. How about fifteen pounds in money and fifteen bushels of spuds? They'll see you through the winter, no trouble. 'Tis all I have. Take it or leave it."

"And a wheelbarrow," added Serjeant, seeing his chance. "You'll need to give me a wheelbarrow."

"What?"

"To carry all those taters in." Serjeant grinned. His teeth were as black as his brother's.

"Done. Go around the back way. I'll meet you there in a few minutes to settle up. What's her name?"

"Rachel Sparrow," interjected Rachel before Serjeant had a chance to speak.

"Well, Rachel Sparrow, strong and tall, come along in the house and meet your mistress. And try to trail no too much dirt across the wife's nice clean floor. She has the strength for cleaning no longer, and so the more mess you make, the more you'll have to tidy."

"Yessuh," said Rachel. The door closed behind her.

I'm trapped, she thought. *Imprisoned in a house of white massas.*

CHAPTER № 5

"You did what?" Eliza Pritchard demanded.

"I gave him fifteen bushels of potatoes, redcoat thief that he is."

"But that's almost all we had stored for the winter. Mr. Pritchard, I despair of you." Eliza Pritchard, Rachel's new missus, went back to her embroidery. A very thin woman, with thin arms, thin face, and thin, straw-like hair, the missus had a greenish, bone-like pallor to her, which made Rachel feel quite sure that she was ill. She was half sitting, half lying in a chair that was almost as long as a bed, and her hands on the piece of fuss-work, as Mamma would have called it, were blue-veined and trembling.

It was hard trying to hate someone who was ill, mighty hard, no matter how Rachel arranged her thinking or tried not to care. Mamma had been ill last year, and Rachel remembered going frantic trying to figure out what would make her better. She wondered if Missus Eliza had the kind of sickness that might heal, as Mamma's had, or whether she would just go on getting sicker till there was nothing left of her.

"I need a cup of water," murmured the missus.

"'Tis what this Nigra's here for. Hey girl, go fetch a drink for your mistress. I'm to the town."

In a second, Jeremiah Pritchard had turned tail and vanished, leaving Rachel and the missus staring at each other. Rachel thought maybe she ought to fetch the water but had no idea where to fetch it from. Besides, she was frozen as a stone. Here she was, in a big dark house that smelled of strangers and sawdust and beef pies, without Titan or Jem or her shawl or the bowl that she ate her cornmeal from. All the dear people and things that made up her life were gone. It was as if she'd been swimming in the cold waters off Cape Roseway and come out of the water to find Birchtown disappeared, and in its place a strange new country that she'd never seen before.

But there was something else, something much worse. Terrible things had happened to her before, but she'd always had Mamma alongside her. She couldn't remember a time when that wasn't the case. Mamma, though she drove Rachel crazy mad with fussing sometimes, was a complete angel. She always knew just the perfect thing to say, though Rachel didn't always understand right away what she was talking about. And she always knew what to do. Now Mamma was gone, maybe forever. And from her last sighting of her, Rachel fathomed that Mamma had been just as scared, just as helpless as Rachel was herself.

"Where's that water?" the mistress asked suddenly. Rachel came to with a shudder, remembering where she was.

"Uh, where should I fetch it from, Missus?" she said at last.

"Never mind that for the moment. Come and stand right here, right in front of me, so I can see you better." Missus looked her up and down. "You're very skinny, your clothes are dirty, your feet are cut and scratched, and you have a big grey stain on your skirt. We'll have to do something about that. Can't have you running around here looking like a beggar. What will respectable people think? Not that it matters too much to me any more."

"That stain'll be from the blueberries. I was collecting them and putting them in my skirt for want of a basket, but I've lost them all now."

"Collecting blueberries? Where do you come from, girl? Who was your master before?"

Rachel swallowed hard. "I didn't have a massa. I'm a free Nigra. I'm not a slave."

"Of course not," said the missus. "We don't have slaves down this way. Or at least we don't say that we do. It's not polite talk. You're a servant, *my* servant now."

It seemed to Rachel that the missus wasn't really listening to her. White folk never did. Nigras could talk and talk till their tongues dried up and fell out of their mouths, but it made no difference. White folk heard only what they wanted to hear or what they said themselves. No Nigra made the slightest dent on their ears. But she reckoned it was worth one more try.

"I live with my Mamma and stepdaddy in Birchtown. I'm not a slave or a servant neither. I'm a free Nigra. I had my certificate of freedom, but Serjeant Gyssop stole it off me." She realized she'd said too much, cringed as though expecting a blow.

But Missus Pritchard only cut a length of purple silk with a tiny pair of scissors, threaded it through a needle, and commenced to sew again. Her hands were so transparent Rachel fancied she could see the veins and bone right through them.

"You'll find the water in a big jug in the back of the house, where we do the cooking. There are cups hanging on the hooks. Bring me a drink, dearie, I'm parched. And then tell me your name—your real name, mind, no fairy stories. Just do as you're told, tell the truth and shame the devil, as they say, and we'll get on very well indeed."

"My name's Rachel, Rachel Sparrow."

"Rachel Sparrow. What a singular name. Are you sure that's it?"

"Yessum. My whole family is called Sparrow except my stepdaddy, Titan. We adopted it as our own on the freedom boat coming here from New York. And Titan says he likes the name well enough and might just take it himself."

The missus was clever enough to ignore the bit about the freedom boat. "Well, if you're a very, very good girl, I may teach you how to write it. Both the Christian name and the last name, Rachel Sparrow."

A missus never taught a slave to read. It was totally unheard of and likely against the law. But if Rachel was shocked, she decided she'd die rather than show it. "I already know how to write my name," she said, marching off with her nose in the air to find the cup.

The missus stared at her in doubt. "I'm not sure this Negro's going to work out," she murmured as she plied her needle. "I'm really not sure at all. She tells such tall tales. Not a *slave*. Lives in *Birchtown* or *Blacktown* or one of those free Negro places. And now she pretends she can *read*. As if she could."

Rachel, on her way to the scullery, heard every word. "R-A-C-H-E-L," she spelled, but too quietly for the missus to overhear. "S-P-A-R-R-O-W. So there!"

It made her feel better for the moment, but then she thought of all the people back home wondering where she was. Titan and Jem (though he was really too little to wonder about anything), Nanna Jacklin and Corey. Soon enough Nathan

Crowley and her friend Ann-Marie would get to hear the news, and they'd be wondering and worrying too. She ached for them all, ached to see and hug them, though she might not dare to hug Nathan. Would they come looking for her? Would they find out where she was?

A big tear rolled down her nose and into her mouth. *Salt,* she thought. *Water. This is just like when the Israelites were slaves in Egypt. Then they crossed the Jordan River and were on their way back to freedom. No matter how bad things are, I have to be brave like them. They got home, and so will I, never mind how much time flows through. Even if I have to wander in the desert for ages and ages.* But there was a pit of loneliness and fear in her belly, and a mountain of doubt in her mind. And Mamma was missing, missing. It was like a chant in her head. *Mamma's missing.* What could be worse than that?

CHAPTER N.º 6

"Missus?" Rachel was dusting the mantel.

"Yes, dearie?"

"Where are we? In which town does this house stand?"

The missus wasn't altogether keen to answer her, not knowing for sure the reason behind the question.

For the first few days she and Rachel had been wary as stray cats of each other. Rachel was scared of the whuppings and hair-pullings that she was sure would arrive soon enough. So far, the missus had been almost too kind. They were nearly the same size, and she'd given Rachel a hardly worn skirt and chemise of her own, with a pair of stout boots besides. But Rachel knew that punishments always came if there were massas and slaves sharing the same house. Titan would say, "That's the way of it, sure enough," and his stepdaughter knew from her own experience that this was true. Although she still felt heartbroken almost to the point of despair, Rachel fetched and carried, she brought water, she scrubbed floors, she slept at the bottom of her missus's bed, and got up in the night whenever needed. She didn't want to feel that tingling slap against her cheek, that pull of the hair that felt like nails driven into her head. She had gotten out of the habit of it.

Meanwhile, the missus had problems of her own with Rachel. She'd never met a slave so hardworking and yet so wicked. Rachel knew how she felt because the missus kept telling her so.

To the missus's mind, Rachel was still uppity as all get-out and told such whoppers of lies her tongue would likely turn blue and fall off. To save the child's immortal soul, the missus preached to her daily about truth-telling being a surefire way to get to Heaven. "Only good Negroes go to Heaven. There is a special place for them, a kind of Black Town of their own. I must tell you this because it is my Christian duty and I have no desire to shirk it," she said, looking weak as white bread lying there on the sofa.

Rachel pitied her on account of her sickness, but she also thought that white folk were always nagging on about their Christian duty in the most two-faced way. Christian duty this, Christian duty that. Be good. Get saved. And yet their Christian duty allowed them to own a slew of slaves and squeeze all the precious freedom out of them, as if they were ripe red apples fresh picked from the trees. Rachel wanted to tell the missus that, wanted to say that being here was like being squeezed dry and useless as an old apple peel, but she kept her mouth clamped. There were just some kinds of things Nigras didn't say to the whites who owned them. It was too risky by a mile.

Instead she asked again, "Which town are we in? Is this Shelburne? It's a mighty big town indeed, and I don't believe I've ever been down this way before."

"Yes," replied the missus, a little concerned. "This is Shelburne. The east side of it. One day, when you stop telling your monstrous fibs and learn how to be a good servant, I may send you on an errand. I need someone I can trust to come and go for me. As you see, it pleases the Lord to keep me sick, too sick to travel for myself, and you can be sure I reflect upon that often enough."

Shelburne! Close to home! Why, she might even meet up with someone she knew. "I promise never to lie again, Missus," Rachel said solemnly, crossing her fingers behind her back. Sometimes fibbing was the only acceptable truth. "I've been a bad, bad girl. Truth is, I'm a slave, er, that is, a servant, sure enough, and I know my place if ever a Nigra did."

The missus smiled, though the smile was weak and had the touch of death in it.

"Well, I'm glad you're set to be good now, dearie, and that you've seen the error of your ways. I thought you'd come round, given enough time in a kind household. Put my 'broidery away for me, the blue silks and the pink—no, not there, in that drawer with the brass handle—and be careful as can be not to catch the scissors on anything, especially not yourself. Later on, after my rest, if you continue beyond reproach, we'll get out a slate and I'll teach you how to spell your name." Her eyes narrowed. "You don't know, do you?"

"No, Missus, never could make head nor tail of them squiggles." Rachel tried to sound as ignorant as possible. "But I sure would be happy for you to learn me. And I like living here with you. You're a real nice missus, right enough."

The missus gave her a sharp look. Perhaps Rachel was laying it on too thick. She needed to tread carefully. "You go to sleep now, Missus, and

I'll bring you a nice drink of milk in your favourite blue cup when you're rested."

"There's my good girl. There's my very good dearie," murmured the missus. In a minute she was fast asleep.

Rachel tiptoed out of the front room, up the stairs, and into the attic, where she couldn't possibly be heard by anyone, not even the massa if he came home suddenly. Then she jumped almost as high as the roof beams and gave an enormous whoop of joy. That devil Serjeant Gyssop had true enough been walking her round in circles just to confuse her. She was a lot nearer Birchtown than she'd ever have reckoned on. And if she played her cards right, to use the massa's words, she'd be out on the street without a chaperone in no time!

CHAPTER №. 7

The massa and missus bickered over Rachel when she was in another room. She could still hear, though. The massa was a harsh man and he would have had her chopping wood, dragging fallen tree trunks away from the property, carrying hefty burdens like a donkey.

"No," the missus insisted. "She's just a girl. You'll use her up."

"She's no but a slave. Slaves are bought to be used up."

"She's a house servant and she does her job more than adequately. I like having her about the place,

I've decided. She keeps me company, and I'm teaching her to read. She's a fast study and is beginning to read to me from my Bible each evening."

"Read, pshaw. You should stop that, 'Liza. You'll be giving her ideas beyond her station. Besides, people will talk."

"I don't have much time on this earth and I'll do what I please, without regard for the neighbours or anyone else except the good Lord. I used to care, but I don't any more. My sickness has made me as fearless as one of God's soldiers. I don't want her wasted on the heavy work, neither. Hire a man for that."

"You've gone plain out of your mind, 'Liza."

"No, I think my sickness has brought me into it. I know what's important now."

"Pshaw," the master said again. He slammed out. Rachel came in.

"Rachel, I can trust you, dearie, can't I?"

"Oh yes, Missus." Rachel bit her lip. She'd been good for a week and was figuring on what would happen now.

"I need you to run an errand into Shelburne for me."

Rachel had guessed right! This was her first, maybe her only chance at freedom. Not that she wanted to lie to the missus or go against her wishes. Not one bit. Much to her own surprise, she found she didn't want to hurt or displease her. After all, Eliza Pritchard, in her sickness and loneliness, grew warmer and more kindly every day. And she stood up for Rachel against the massa. She'd become more like a dear old aunt than a slave owner. But Rachel needed to get herself, or at least a message, home to her family. It was vital to let them know where she was. They were still the important ones. Their sorrow at losing her had to be uppermost in her mind.

"But first of all, thread this needle for me," said the missus. "I can't seem to get the silk through the eye. It's *my* eyes, I'm afraid. They're dimming fast."

Indeed, she seemed to be dimming all over and could barely lift her hand to sew. "Into her last fade," Mamma would have said. "Seein' Heav'n sure enough, but not too much earth, with all them angels flowerin' and flutterin' round her."

CHAPTER N°. 8

An hour later Rachel was on her way, with a basket and directions to the store. It turned out to be the same store that she'd visited with her tuppence when she'd lived in Shelburne in the long gone Maybe House. The store was painted blue, with little diamonds of glass over the door. And there were still the luscious smells of apples and maple sugar. And the barrels of salt fish. And the coils of rope and fishing tackle. And the selfsame horrid lady serving, the one who wrinkled her nose like there was a bad smell under it when Rachel stood in front of her. Oh, how could Rachel have forgotten that? A dozen frightening thoughts came rushing into her head like a hurricane. But dressed in her new chemise and skirt, with her fine leather boots and shiny clean face, Rachel was a heap more respectable than the first time she'd come calling. Just knowing that gave her a lick of confidence.

"Good morning." She smiled. "I'm the servant of Missus Eliza Pritchard."

The woman, who was stacking loaves of bread on the counter, paid no attention to Rachel.

"Good morning," she repeated a little louder, her teeth a mite clenched under her grin. "I'm the servant of—"

"I heard you the first time. Slave you mean, not servant. Right?"

"Yessum." Rachel's shoulders fell. This sure was a miserable woman to deal with. *Odious,* the missus would call her, *odious* and *venomous.* Missus Pritchard knew a trunkful of excellent words, which she unfolded on suitable occasions. Rachel refolded them and packed them back in her own trunk as fast as she could for later remembrance.

"Well, what is it you want? I don't have all day for the likes of you, you know. Spit it out."

"Please'um, my missus says could she have a dozen of the new-picked sour apples as she has the craving for them, a skein of violet silk, and do you have any fabric fit to make me a coat, as winter will be coming on soon? She said to put everything on account, and Massa Pritchard will be in to pay for my buyings directly."

"Humph." The woman plonked down the skein of silk, which she'd pulled from a drawer. Rachel's hand shot out fast and grabbed it as though scared to get a swipe on the knuckles. However, the shopkeeper was already on her way to the back of the store to count out apples, her striped skirt swishing along the floor as she walked.

"Tell your missus there'll be Negro material coming in next week or so that'll make a passable slave coat. I don't have any other fabric at present, except what's good enough for God-fearing white folk."

"Yessum."

"And don't you touch anything else on that counter." Rachel stepped back fast.

The woman returned and filled her basket with the small green fruit. It might be sour, but Rachel's mouth watered all the same.

"Now you get away home, do you hear? And give my best to Mrs. Pritchard. I heard tell she's not a well woman."

"Yessum, thank you." Rachel began to angle towards the door. She moved more and more slowly, like a tortoise without a head, as Mamma would have said. But she was thinking fast. From here she could try to run home to Birchtown. She could find her way well enough through the forest west of the town and around the bay. But no doubt the massa would follow and find her, maybe track her with dogs, bringing a heap of trouble down on the whole family. She'd heard stories of beatings and burnings when slaves had misbehaved, even here. There just had to be another option.

Touching her hand to the doorknob, she took a great gulp of a breath and turned. "There's just one more thing. The missus wants me to run an errand to the Crowley household, and I've forgotten the address."

"You Negro girls haven't the wits of a pigeon. It's on King Street, second-to-last house before the water. Got that?"

"Yessum."

The woman suddenly looked suspicious. "Haven't I seen you somewhere before?"

"No'um. Never." With the apples bobbing up and down, jostling one another and the silk skein in her basket, Rachel fled.

It took all the pluck she had to make her way to Nathan's house, her feet dragging like they had iron chains on them. Once she finally arrived, it took at least a minute for her to get up the courage to knock on the door.

Please let it be Nathan, please, please, she thought as she heard footsteps. But it was Hannah the house slave and not Nathan who appeared. She came out of the house to fetch an armful of chopped wood and stopped dead in her tracks when she saw Rachel standing in front of her.

"They Nigras all searchin' for you," she said, her eyes so round they looked about to pop out of her head. "You and you Mamma. They say mebbe you fall in Port Roseway and wash away into the great sea. My, Rachel, you sure do dress nice nowadays."

"Hannah, I haven't time for this. Listen to me, will you?"

The girl nodded, rather sorrowfully, Rachel thought. No doubt she wanted a chance to chatter.

"Tell Nathan, tell Nathan Crowley, to go down to Birchtown and tell Titan I'm living with the Pritchards out at the east end of Shelburne. Tell Nathan to let Titan know they've taken me as their slave."

"Their slave? They never did."

"Yes, they did, and you must tell. Do you understand?"

"Oh, no, Rachel. It be more than my skin worth to say stories like that to white folk."

"You can, and you must. You hear me? Nathan will thank you for it."

"All right. I try." Hannah looked more sorrowful than ever.

"And tell Nathan to tell Titan that Massa Pritchard's a mighty strict man, and he should be careful. Understand?"

"I guess." Hannah stared at her toes. Then she drew a circle in the earth with her foot, picked up the firewood, and sloped indoors with it.

Could the girl be trusted to speak to Nathan Crowley? Could she even be trusted to remember? Rachel couldn't be sure. And she hadn't a clue whether Nathan would have the pluck to go back into Birchtown with things as they were, the Nigras and the whites having taken so against each other. But there wasn't a skim of time left to waste wondering. She had to get back to the Pritchards with her basket of apples before Missus 'Liza realized something was amiss.

CHAPTER N.º 9

The missus was growing sicker by the day.
And as she grew sicker, she grew even kinder.
She fed Rachel the same food the family ate. She
continued, when not too tired, to teach her how
to read. And she always spoke softly and tenderly to
her. Rachel, despite everything, despite her suspicion of white folk, was coming to love her.
She'd never been treated so fine and fondly by a
white person, not even Nathan Crowley. But
she was afraid for when the missus died. The massa
was stern as a white preacher, and she didn't want
to be left alone with him. He raised his eyebrows

and his voice whenever he saw Rachel and the missus together. And he always spoke to his wife as though Rachel weren't in the room, as if she were a table or a footstool, an unfeeling thing.

"'Tis not fitting you should treat a slave that way. Give her the scraps off our plates and send her to sleep in the barn. The weather's warm enough. She'll no freeze. I'm no for wasting my money, my food, and my fuel on a slave."

The missus spoke very quietly. Every breath was an effort to her. "She prepares our meals and feeds me the very food I need with a spoon. How could I deny her her own share? And I need her by me at night. Dying is a lonely thing, and with you sleeping in your study, she's a great comfort to me. Almost like a daughter, in fact."

"You go mad in your sickness, 'Liza, as I said before. But I'll no interfere. 'Tis said one should humour the sick and no give them more grief than 'tis theirs already." Just then there was a knock on the front door. "Since you need your slave girl with you," he sneered, "best I go answer it."

The massa was not gone a minute when he started to shout. "Get out of here," he was yelling. "And make sure you no come back with your lies. She's my slave fair and square, as Serjeant Gyssop said, and I've had a bill of sale drawn up to prove it."

Neither Rachel nor the mistress could hear a response. They stared at each other in consternation.

"Go, Rachel, and find out what's happening," the missus bade her at last, as the massa started yelling again.

Rachel, her heart pounding, crept to the front door and, crouching behind the massa, saw her own dear Titan, tall and gangly, standing there. So Hannah had told Nathan after all, and Nathan had fetched him. How hard it must have been for them to do what they did, and how brave they both were. Rachel scarce believed it. The sight of her stepdaddy was like taking powerful medicine to cure a sickness.

Titan was no good at talking. He was a strong and silent man whose hands and feet, with their missing toes, worked much harder than his mouth, so he only had a few words to use up every day. But today he kept repeating quietly: "She's not a slave. She's a free Nigra. She's my stepdaughter and I want her back." Rachel had never heard him make such a long speech in her life, and she loved him for it.

"Get!" shouted the massa, raising his hand.

"I'll go to court if need be," Titan threatened.

Nigras never won in court. It was a bad idea and brought all kinds of trouble on their heads— even a murder, once, that Rachel knew of. It was talked of in Birchtown all the time. And, as if everything weren't frightening enough, the massa was now reaching for his long-barreled gun, which stood behind the front door.

In a trice, Rachel knew what she had to do. She rushed between the two men and grabbed Titan's hand. It felt warm and reassuring. How she'd ached for this moment. She'd imagined it a hundred times at night while attending to the missus. How he'd come for her, how she'd return with him, how Mamma would already be back at home, and how they'd all live together once more with Jem. But now, though it almost broke her spirit, she had to send her stepdaddy away.

"Titan," she said, "I'm all right. I can manage. Don't worry your head about me."

"Rachel." He stared at her in astonishment. "You're here. I'll go to court. I'll get you back."

"No. Listen. I want to be with you, you know that. You're my family and I love you more than anything. But the missus is very kind to me, I promise. She's very sick and frightened, too. She needs someone to tend her and I'm all there is. I *have* to stay here."

"Listen to what the girl says. She's no as stupid as I thought," grinned the massa, setting down the gun.

"No, Rachel," cried Titan, totally bewildered. He sounded as if his heart were being torn in half.

"Yes, Titan. Let it be for the moment," she whispered, hoping the massa wouldn't hear what she was about to say next. "When the time comes, when the missus is in Heaven with the angel choirs, as Mamma says, we'll find a way." She let go of his hand and backed away indoors.

"Where is your mamma? Is she with you?" Titan called out after her.

"No. I don't know where Mamma is. I don't know at all." She wanted to add Mamma was enslaved to George Gyssup but was afraid to in front of the massa. He might give her a good whupping. Now she was crying something dreadful. She couldn't believe she'd told Titan to go. She couldn't believe Mamma was still lost. Tears streamed down her cheeks as she stumbled back to the sitting room.

"What on earth is going on out there?" asked the missus, upset herself at the sight of Rachel's tears. Between sobs Rachel managed to tell her.

"So you really aren't a slave," the missus mused. "You were telling the truth all along."

"Yessum. I always tell the truth when I can. Now you can see by my stepdaddy coming after me I was right."

The missus said nothing more, but Rachel could tell she was storing the new knowledge in her mind. Perhaps one day she'd take it out like a mint sixpence, turn it over in her palm, and buy Rachel a whole new life with it.

CHAPTER Nº 10

The missus had grown weak as a kitten.
She couldn't even take gruel from Rachel's
spoon. The doctor came from the town, looked
at her lying there on her sofa, and shook his
head. That was the way of it with doctors. Rachel
remembered from the plantation. They came,
they felt the pulse of their patients, and they
shook their heads. It meant either they didn't
know what was wrong or there was no hope at
all. Usually it meant both.

Micmac medicine was a heap more powerful—it had healed Rachel's own mamma less

than a year back—but she couldn't see these white folks agreeing to swallow any of it. She'd mentioned it to the missus once, but the missus had shaken her head, too, just like the doctor. "Nothing will save me now, child. We must make the best of things as they are."

After the doctor had gone, the missus called the massa in. "Stay where you are, Rachel," she whispered as Rachel turned to go out. "I want you to hear this. Jeremiah, I'm dying."

The massa sighed. "Yes, Eliza, I'm no ignorant of that. I'm sorry for it, I am indeed. You've been a good wife to me, despite your strange fancies. But this is a harsh climate for an Englishwoman."

"I have a dying wish, husband."

The massa sighed again. Dying wishes were sacred. Even Rachel knew that.

"I want you to send Rachel home. I would say I want you to manumit her—free her from slavery—but she's no slave."

The massa put his hands in his pockets and his round face turned red as a harvest moon. "I paid good money for her, Eliza, as you well know, and gave Gyssop all our potatoes for the winter. It'll be harder than ever now to get through the lean season, since the government's reduced our rations."

"All the more reason to let her go. Serjeant Gyssop fooled you, Jeremiah Pritchard. He *fooled* you. No wonder he's never seen about town any more. He plucked the girl from her family, *stole* her, and he sold her where he had no right to."

The massa's hands balled into fists and his face turned more crimson than ever, but he said nothing.

"He sold her *illegally,*" the missus went on, using the long, harsh word to push the truth home.

"Now hang on, Eliza. That's no fair. She's our Nigra, fair and square."

The missus, losing her remaining strength, started to gasp. "She's a free Negro . . . who has cared for me and worked for us . . . for nothing.

You are to give her five guineas . . . for her labour . . . and let her go."

"*No!*" the massa shouted. He made a move towards Rachel and she cringed, afraid he was about to strike her.

But the missus spoke again. "Listen to me . . . and don't take out your anger and frustration on the girl. She has done nothing wrong . . . It is we who have done wrong."

"This is too much, Eliza. Your sickness has affected your mind."

"You are to give her five guineas . . . Jeremiah . . . and let her go," repeated the missus. "This is my dying wish . . . as God is my witness. Rachel, dearie . . . you've been like a daughter . . . to me . . . my dear. I wish you . . . well."

The massa, not for the first time, stormed out of the room.

CHAPTER N° 11

It was fall now, a cool, breezy day. Rachel, who had walked all night, feeling her way along the half-familiar path, stood on the crest of a hill, staring down. The last time she'd come by this way, it had been summer. Some of the tall trees were waxing a deep, dark gold, casting their brilliant shadows along the ground. They looked different now she was free again, now she truly understood what freedom meant.

She couldn't see Birchtown yet, couldn't make out the little settlement of Negroes, but she could already smell the wood-fires burning in the stoves and fireplaces and even the pit-cabins below. She knew Titan was down there working, sawing a piece of wood or knocking a nail into their new house. Jem, her tiny brother, was down there too. And Nanna Jacklin, and little Corey, who used to drive her crazy. She couldn't wait to hug him, to hug them all. They were really one big family, and she had come back to them.

Only Mamma was still missing, and that was a great sorrow, but now at least she could tell Titan about Gyssup, and Rachel prayed that when the time came they would find her, too.

She stood for another minute, thinking of Missus Eliza. She had been a good, kind woman. Rachel would carry the memory of her every-where she went, just as if the missus were one of her relations.

The girl walked down the hill slowly, the forest a hazy jumble of shade and sun, a magical quilt of nature. The coat over her arm would keep her warm, the coins in her pouch would see her whole family through the winter. She jingled

them softly. The massa had frowned as he counted out every one of them, but in the end he hadn't stinted. He was afeard, he muttered, that his wife would come back to haunt him.

It was time to pick the cranbetties, Rachel thought suddenly, imagining the red, sour berries on her tongue. There had been frost, and they would have come ripe while she was away. Like her adventure with the Pritchards, they were seemingly bitter, but with a curious aftertaste of sweetness.

Still, first things first. She would see to the work of picking tomorrow. In five minutes she would be home.

BOOK FOUR

An Elephant Tree
Christmas

CHAPTER N°1

"All this work," sniffed Rachel. *"You'd* never think there'd be so much of it in such a narrow little dark place. I spend all my time huffing and puffing." She dragged a kettle of water to the fire. It sloshed sideways, so she dispersed some of the spillage around the floor with her bare foot. Droplets raced across the wooden boards like ants, vanishing double-quick into corners. It was almost as good as sweeping, she persuaded herself, which she didn't have the time or inclination for right now.

Here they lived, Rachel and Titan and Jem in

their new hut, a small log cabin down by the shore of Birchtown. Titan hadn't given up after their disaster in Shelburne. He had fashioned every log and seam of this new home himself. It wasn't the Maybe House, it could never be that, but it was a kind of house all the same, with one small room and a fireplace to cook on and keep them passably warm—as long as there was enough wood chopped. Rachel felt she mustn't be ungrateful—it was much better than the pit-cabin, anything had to be better than that—but sometimes it was hard to keep the tears from squeezing out and running down her nose when her hands were rough and aching from the labour of it all.

Mamma was still lost, and Rachel felt lost without her. It wasn't just a question of love. And it wasn't just that Mamma was the twine that tied them neatly into a family bundle. It was more than that. Truth told, Rachel found it dreadfully hard being the mamma in Mamma's place, doing all the woman chores and looking after the baby besides. Though she'd never have admitted it before, it was even harder not to hear Mamma's grumping day after day. The lack of it meant her warm stout presence was gone and Rachel was supposed to act the grown-up woman of the house. Now it was just Titan and herself to guard Jem against the harsh befallings of the world.

She didn't feel ready for it. She wanted normal child chores and the freedom to be out in the woods with her Micmac friend, Ann-Marie, or even better, she wanted to be sitting on a rock, book-studying. Or putting memorized tricky things into little Corey's head, reading and arithmetic, to make Nanna Jacklin's grandson into a civilized Nigra. She needed to give those tricks away, pass them along like a great chain of learning. First to Corey, then to her own little brother, Jem, when he was big enough, and then, who knew? Learning, reading and writing, could just stretch and stretch like a great fishing net till it covered the world. And everyone fished up in that net would be happier for it, doubtless.

Thinking about Mamma again, Rachel went over it all in her mind, just as she'd done nearly every day since Mamma had been gone. She'd racked and riddled her brains and told Titan all she knew. Rachel was a good describer. But no one, not Titan, not Nathan Crowley, not even the Sunday preacher who came sometimes to Birchtown but travelled around the whole area, had been able to search Mamma or her captor, George Gyssop, out. Now the Micmac family of Ann-Marie were seeking. They used their wits and their eyes and small bunches of herbs and stones to divine by, but though it was said that they could find anyone or anything, that they could find a lone white crab in the whole wide ocean, they'd not found Mamma. Maybe Gyssop had moved on, taking her with him, his property.

Rachel tried to remember more. Her missus Pritchard in Shelburne had said George Gyssop was likely named after King George of England, but a man less like a king you'd be hard put to find.

"You've done your best. That's the truth," replied Titan, when she told him that last tidbit of knowledge, and there was the end to it. But he had a wild lost look, and every night he sat with his arms dangling and his chin dropped almost all the way to his chest.

The hut had chinks in the log walls, filled with straw, bits of paper, and scraps of fabric the family had found to keep the wind out. There wasn't much thrown away in Birchtown. Almost every last fragment of anything was used up. Yet there were still gaps in the walls for the gale, when it visited, to whistle through. This wasn't entirely bad. A space between two logs near the door made a bit of a hidey-hole for keeping things in. Rachel thought of it as her treasure trove. Not that she had a pile of things to store there. But she did have something special: the five English guineas. Rachel had pushed the precious coins under some straw in the hole, wanting to keep them for the worst days of winter. Then they'd shine like summer sun. Then they'd be more useful than a spade to dig taters, more useful even than the biggest basket in the world for *bluebetties,* and then some. She didn't tell anyone about them, not Ann-Marie, not Titan, not Nathan Crowley. They were her secret.

Rachel had never seen nor known such money in her life before. Each heavy drop of gold was worth twenty-one shillings, more than she could carry in her hand at one time or fold her mind around. She tried doing the sums, using the numbers that Nathan had taught her. One guinea was a nest egg; five a fortune, likely more than Titan could earn in half a year—and that was if there was work for him. There'd been little enough lately, skilled carpenter though he was.

Sometimes Rachel caught a glint of the hidden coins in the straw of the wall, especially after the wind blew hard, and covered them fast, her fingers trembling and dark against the spangly cool yellowness of them. They were a secret spell. They lifted the Sparrows from the level of the other Nigras roundabout and set them somewhere else. In their way they were now high and mighty maybe as Colonel Blucke, the head of Birchtown. Thinking that made her feel guilty and good at the same time—she was keeping something back from Titan, it was true, but in the end it would be something for all of them. Her coins were the guinea promise. They drifted luminous and spanking clean through her dreams. Somehow she imagined they would keep the family safe from the bad people that still hung around Birchtown, the de-listed soldiers and the homeless drifters. She didn't know where those folk came from. She didn't know what they kept locked up in their minds. It frightened her.

But, "Here we are, Titan," she was finally going to say one day around Christmas, her chest puffed like a pigeon, if things became too hard to bear. "Here's all we need to buy the fish and grain to get us through these mis'rable times."

And Titan would stare at her and grin, and they'd all dance round in a circle, singing and laughing. Negro frolicks, the white folk would call their antics, with that lordly toss of the head. But Rachel knew better. It was just pure energy that needed to be let out, like steam from the cooking pot, and a bit of the fear as well. Best of all, when Rachel came to think back on it, Mamma was in those imaginings too, singing and laughing with the rest of them.

The new Sparrow hut was a little ways along from the big rich house of Colonel Blucke, and Titan always tipped his cap to him of a morning, especially as Colonel Blucke had loaned him tools to make their new hut. Colonel Blucke wasn't white or black. He was somewhere in between, a nice tan colour like he was white folk sunned too long, and that made him special. He'd been mighty important during the war, an army officer in charge of many Nigras. A kind man, though gruff enough to put the shyness into Rachel whenever she passed him, he still organized the men into work brigades whenever possible and bargained with the white authorities back in Shelburne over food and pay. But all Colonel Blucke's effort didn't seem to help a titch at the moment. Rations were cut, the Nigras were facing more starvation than they'd ever borne as slaves, and you could actually hear winter most days, whining round corners and rattling ill-fitting doors. Or even worse, pit-cabin roofs. "I'm coming," it seemed to be moaning. "You think things are bad now, but I'm coming, so watch out."

Rachel prayed it wouldn't be like last winter. The snow had been piled so high it covered the whole town, and all she'd seen when she went out were rows of spiralling smoke, issuing out of the ice—like men were puffing on their tobaccy pipes underneath. That was because the drifts had grown so tall all the chimneys and roof holes were hidden. Folk both black and white crossed themselves or spat sideways when they spoke of it. They prayed such cruel weather would never come again. But if it did there were still those five guineas. There were always the guineas. Come snow or hail or freezing weather too bad to tramp out in, the Sparrows would make it through the ice days. But Rachel didn't want the coins used up faster than needed, for after that there'd be nothing. And the feeling of having nothing made a big hurting hole in her middle like the worst kind of bellyache. So she had to figure out, careful as a squirrel hoarding for its long sleep, when and how to act, what to use the sparkling money for.

CHAPTER №2

"My turn to tell a story," smiled Ann-Marie. It was one of those strange mild days in late fall that squeezed themselves, flat and miraculous, between one sharp edge of wintry weather and another. Rachel wasn't exactly sitting listening, she didn't have the leisure for that, but she was spreading damp cleaning rags and Jem's few washed bits of clothes on a sun-warmed rock while cocking an ear to what her best friend was saying. It was so good to be together again, so good to see Ann-Marie smile, even if Rachel did have to work all the while.

It's amazing, she thought, *how many things you can do at the same time if you only put your mind to it.* Flat lengths of bark full of drying *cranbetties* lay in the sun, and angular wooden logs, with pale glistening edges that leaked slightly, stood heaped against the hut. Rachel had laid out the berries and then split the wood this morning against the cold that would no doubt pay another visit soon. Next time it came calling it would likely stay till spring, spreading out its snowy petticoats and settling in like the lady of a great house. She winced at the thought. Ann-Marie had helped her pile up the firewood, meanwhile explaining how berries could be crushed and dried with slivers of meat, maybe using wood smoke for the drying process, to make winter food.

"I don't think there'll ever be much meat in this house," replied Rachel sorrowfully. She hadn't eaten a bite of beef since returning from the Pritchards'. Then she thought of the guineas, each about the size of a man's thumbnail. "Broad pieces," she'd heard them called, but they looked anything but broad to her. Perhaps she could buy a whole cow with the coins and then there'd be milk and meat. But she knew it wasn't the best way to spend them. Cows had to be fed, after all. And once you'd eaten the meat there'd be no more milk. That was the way of things, sure enough, as Titan would say.

"Story, story," cried Corey, who was hanging around as usual, doing nothing that could be called useful. "But no more spider stories, please." He was still an annoyance, but it was a gladness to Rachel that he said *please* and that he was beginning to speak properly. Perhaps something could be done with him after all.

"Kisiku'k wikuombk ..." began Ann-Marie.

"What's that mean?" Corey demanded. Two or three other Nigra children had crept close to hear. Jem, who had hauled himself upright, was hanging on to Ann-Marie's shoulder as she sat on the ground cross-legged. A bit wobbly on his feet, he was staring straight into her face, concentrating. He was also drooling, with all the new teeth coming through. Looking around her, Rachel suddenly had an idea: this would make a good learning group. Another time, when Ann-Marie wasn't storytelling, perhaps Rachel could teach the Nigra children that letters might have horns or curlicues or look like broken splinters of wood, but when it came right down to it, they all meant something important.

Colonel Blucke marched by, actually tipping *his* hat to *them,* rather than the other way round, as if they were grown-up important people. Not that most of them had hats, of course.

"Good mornin', Colonel Blucke," chorused the children, who had been taught on all accounts to be polite to him. But the colonel had already disappeared into his big house.

"Kisiku'k wikuombk ... it's how we begin a story. It tells how everyone is sitting listening. That might be a lesson for *you,*" Ann-Marie told Corey, who was flexing his toes, worrying an ant, and scratching his head. "It's not another spider story, don't worry, nor the story of Rabbit and

Moon, though that will be good for another time. It's a child story."

There was a rustle in the small stand of trees above the shore, perhaps folk coming through, but for the moment Rachel paid little heed, though she felt a quick squeeze of the heart. New Nigras were always crossing and recrossing Birchtown, tramping down to the shore or through the forests with a kind of longing in them. Times were bad, Nigras were unwanted over in Shelburne, and so men and women were forever looking for a staying place. If she got mixed up with them, with their hoping and wanting, she'd soon be thinking more about their troubles than those of her own family. So she was growing hard. Her eyes would glitter when she saw the ragtag strangers, perhaps from frozen tears, but she'd ignore both her tears and the people. They always had a certain set to their shoulders, like they were being pulled down into the earth, life being too heavy for them, but there was nothing she could do about it.

"There was, in the old times, an old woman and an old man," Ann-Marie began. "They were very poor. One day they heard a great banging from under the earth and went to see what it was. A tiny hand came up and they yanked on it, hard, hard, till a little boy burst up through the ground like a young shrub."

"Was he from a pit-cabin?" asked one of the Nigra girls, whose nickname was Molasses because her face was always sticky. She lived in a little pit-cabin herself, her family was that poor.

"Kind of. He was from the middle of the earth. A spirit place."

"I bet the old man and the old woman were mighty surprised," said Rachel.

Another rustle. She stared up at the trees for a moment but could see nothing. Maybe it wasn't Nigra folk after all, but a bear or a wolf in the pines. Or even worse, a de-listed soldier. The small circle of children harkening to the Indian story were safe enough here. They could run inside the Sparrow hut and bolt the door if threatened, though it would make for a massive crowd. There was always one kind of danger or another. *Calm yourself, girl,* she told herself in Mamma's voice. She was too fanciful for her own good.

"Mighty surprised," replied Ann-Marie, who had noticed nothing amiss, "but however poor you are, you can't just throw away children. So they took him home and looked after him. He grew very fast, as boys always do, and the old man and the old woman, who became poorer and poorer with each passing day, had a great deal of trouble feeding him."

The children nodded. This was something they understood.

There was definitely something in those trees, and Rachel felt that whatever it might be was aimed directly at her, or at them all, maybe. That was the way her imagination worked. A dark cloud darted across the sun like an arrow spun from a bow, and she clenched her fists. Ann-Marie looked up, mildly surprised.

"Something wrong?" she murmured.

"Not sure," Rachel whispered back. She turned to the children. There were at least fifteen of them now, too many to fit into the hut. They'd drifted by, two or three at a time, eager to hear the Micmac story. "I think we should save the rest of this tale for another day. Is it a good place to stop, Ann-Marie?"

"A very good place." Ann-Marie took her cue from Rachel. "Can you imagine what's going to happen next?" she asked the children. They shook their heads.

"Maybe I'll start to teach you Nigras your letters next time we meet," Rachel went on. "Till it gets too cold, this can be our schoolhouse, right by this big bush. Ann-Marie can tell tales, I can teach reading and writing, and Corey—" Rachel stared at the grubby child with disapproval "—will show us all how to wash our faces and comb our hair. We could meet every second day except church day."

"Aw, I wanna hear rest of story now." Corey rubbed his nose. "I don' wanna wait."

"Time is jus' an arm long. You can reach clean across it." Rachel was borrowing one of Mamma's mysterious sayings. There was never any arguing with what Mamma said. Most folk didn't understand her anyhow, though she sounded fancy. Rachel thought the saying might just shut Corey up, and it did, though he commenced to scratch his head again. "You all go home now," continued Rachel. She said goodbye to Ann-Marie, picked up Jem, and hurried into the house, shutting the door. She really didn't want to know who or what was in those trees.

CHAPTER N° 3

It didn't take her long to find out. Five minutes or so later there came a hard impatient knocking at the door.

"It's a person, then, that's for sure. Bears and wolves don't knock." But she made no move to open it.

Titan was out on a rare day of carpentering, and she was all alone with Jem. It could be a white soldier, looking to make some mischief. She shuddered. She'd had her fill of *them*.

The banging grew more insistent. "Who's there?" she cried, her voice wavy as a swath of seaweed.

"It's me, Rachel, Nathan Crowley. Could you please open the door? Way things are, with Nigras hating whites and vice versa, this bain't the best place to be."

Greatly relieved, Rachel drew up the latch. "You should say, 'It is I,' not, 'It's me,'" she corrected, unable to resist, as soon as she saw him. Theirs was a who-could-best-whom kind of friendship. "That's what you taught me."

"Oh, for heaven's sake. This is important. You want to hear, or d'you prefer to go on correcting my grammar?" He ducked into the house.

"Mamma?" she breathed. "Is it Mamma? Have you found her?"

"No, this is not about your mother. It's about … Hannah."

"Hannah?" Hannah was the Crowleys' slave. What had she to do with Rachel?

There was a slight rustle, like the noise in the trees earlier. Nathan glanced sideways and back, gave a short whistle, and Hannah crept over from her hiding place. "We there, Miz Rachel, in them trees, watchin' you with they children." A sorry sight, Hannah, tired-eyed and bedraggled, slouched behind Nathan, her face peeping round his left shoulder.

What were they doing here together? What on earth was the matter? Rachel couldn't believe Missus Crowley would allow her slave to go gallivanting through the wild lands between Shelburne and Birchtown. She had duties at home. Then she realized: Hannah was carrying a small damp bundle wrapped in a rag, as though she were free to be journeying.

"She fell in a stream," Nathan offered helpfully, as if this explained everything. "I fished her out."

"'Tweren't my fault, Massa Nathan. It black as hell in that there forest."

Rachel looked from one to the other of them with amazement, and Jem climbed up and hugged Nathan's knees.

"What are you both doing here?" Rachel asked finally, fit to burst with curiosity. "Did something dreadful happen? Did your house burn down?"

"My parents turned Hannah out."

"What?"

"Times are bad, our rations have been cut, and many owners are getting rid of their slaves before winter comes. They're all over the streets of Shelburne. My parents say they won't be able to feed Hannah and us as well, so they're letting her go."

"I free, Miz Rachel." Hannah sounded doleful as a dog on a wet and windy day.

Rachel, in return, was speechless as a duck with all its quacks used up. This didn't seem like a good kind of free.

After staring at his silver-buckled shoes for a moment and taking care to meet nobody's gaze, Nathan took Rachel aside and whispered to her, "I know things are hard, but could she stay here?"

"How're we expected to afford her keep if your rich family can't?" she whispered back. "Our rations, what there were of them, have been cut too." She would have hated for Hannah to hear her, but it had to be said.

"I don't know. But with no family, with no logic or wit about her, the girl won't survive on her own for long."

That was true enough. Although it bruised Rachel's brain to think badly of her, Hannah didn't have the sense of a flea, had actually liked being a slave.

"D'you have any money?" Rachel asked Hannah. "Did they pay you off?" She almost added, "Like Massa Pritchard paid me," but stopped herself just in time. Best not to go sliding over that cliff.

"No'um. They say, 'You free now. Hannah. Look what we done for you. Take you baggage and go.' But I don' have no baggage."

"Nothing at all?"

"Only what I standin' up in, Miz Rachel, and this here little bundle, wi' a crust of bread in it. I bet it all wet now." Hannah wasn't standing up in much, a chemise and dust-stained skirt, no shoes. Nathan had the grace to look ashamed.

"Do *you* have any money?" Rachel asked him.

"No. Only my pocket money, and I spent that on maple-sugar apples before I knew this was going to happen."

"Maple-sugar apples. Huh. Some people don't know they're born, sure enough." Rachel felt higher and mightier than Nathan Crowley for a moment. Times might be hard, but he still spent his coins on candy. Then she looked at both him and Hannah in despair. This problem would take a mountain of chewing over. She thought and she thought, her mind arguing with itself like white folks and Nigras having a quarrel. Suddenly she had a glimmer of an idea. "Go into that corner, both of you, and warm your hands by the fire."

"I'm not cold," Nathan said testily.

"Never mind. Take yourself over there and do as you're told." In the past Rachel could never have imagined speaking like this to Nathan. But somehow now, as an extension of his mean family, he didn't deserve better. And she wasn't done yet. "Whatever you do, don't turn your head around, for I've a lifesaver of a plan. You neither, Hannah. Keep your eyes glued on those embers."

"Yessum." Hannah scuttled across to the fire-place, Jem crawling after her. To Rachel's relief, Nathan followed, his head down. Sometimes whites couldn't think up any better schemes than Nigras, it appeared, though they had a heap more schooling.

As soon as she was sure neither of them was watching, Rachel darted over to her hidey-hole. She shifted a bit of straw, her heart hammering. But there they still were, precious and untouched, her very own guineas, small and round and golden. They glittered in the narrow bar of sun that shone in a white blaze through the door. Almost unwillingly, loath to touch it, knowing it would be a parting touch, she took one of them out. It glittered in her palm and she grasped it tightly. Four. Now there would be four. She covered the others. There was still a great store of money to get the Sparrow family through the winter.

"Nathan, look here." She unclasped her hand.

He stared at the small coin in wonder. "A broad piece. A King George guinea. More than I ever had. Where in heaven or earth did you get that?"

"Never you mind. It's my money. I got it fair and square." She'd learned that phrase from Serjeant Gyssop. His shadow passed over her and she shivered as she said it. There was a moment's hush as they all stared at the guinea, Hannah's eyes near popping out of her head. Then Rachel spoke again. "I want you to take this coin, Nathan, and use it for us. Every so often you're to go to the store of that nasty white woman—the one who looks like she has a bad smell under her nose—in Shelburne, and bring food here for the winter."

"Why don't you do it? You're the one with all the money." Nathan sounded snotty.

"I can't. She won't serve me if I don't have a white massa. Don't fetch nothing fancy, just pota-toes and meal and other fill-the-belly kinds of food. That way I can tell Titan that Hannah is living here but you're looking out for her. That way he'll be thinking she's not costing us a penny nor a three-penny piece. It's our only hope."

Nathan promised. And that only left Titan to go along with having Hannah live with them. They argued that night. Titan couldn't understand why the Crowleys would have a slave but keep her somewhere else.

"I not a slave no more. I free," Hannah moaned.

Titan looked at her sharply, but Rachel had practised her answer over and over again. "The Crowleys had no room for her. It's just that Nathan Crowley feels guilty, and he knows we're poor, so he's helping out."

"Harrumph." Titan was beginning to sound like Mamma. But as he muttered nothing else, just sat in his rickety chair, pushing it onto its two back legs with his eyes shut, Rachel took it they had a deal.

Hannah was a rare nuisance to have around. She was like a shadow Rachel couldn't shake. But the girl did carry Jem around on her hip, and she did bank the fire, and she did help with all the other chores, and that, Rachel felt, was maybe worth a hundred guineas in the scheme of things. But she had to get Hannah to stop saying "Miz Rachel" and "Yessum" all the time. It made Rachel feel like a slave owner.

CHAPTER N⁰ 4

"What a crowd!" Rachel exclaimed with a mix of gladness and dread as she went outside. She more or less had to drag Hannah with her. Hannah didn't believe in "the book-learnin'" for slaves or ex-slaves or Nigras in general. She thought "them things" too uppity. But she'd come anyway, to hang on to Jem and make sure he didn't get in the way. Maybe, with a little luck and a lot of trying, some tiddly-bit of knowledge would squirm its way into her brain.

The day was real nippy, but a bunch of children were there anyhow, waiting by the big bush outside the Sparrow hut. Rachel had given maybe five lessons so far, and word had spread like beef fat on bread. There must have been about thirty children now, all eager for stories and lessons. It was pretty amazing, but a mite daunting too, all those pairs of eyes fixed on hers and expecting so much from her. Rachel wondered if she had enough learning stored in her brain for them, but she was bent on teaching them whatever she knew. Still, there wouldn't be too many more days of class, for there was already frost on the ground and the snow would come soon. It hung like a great grey-white sheet over Birchtown, ready to drop down and cover the land. Many of the Nigra children had no coats or shoes. As it was they sat huddled against each other for warmth, their small faces bleak. The makeshift school would have to stop for the winter and that would be a great pity. Because learning was freedom. Rachel had drummed it into them till their ears burned, and not with cold neither.

Ann-Marie had come today and was just about to finish her story. She was hurrying it along so that Rachel would have time to teach another batch of her curlicue letters or numbers before the snow enveloped the little gathering. It was already beginning to spill out of the sky, plump flakes light and white as goose feathers.

"So," said Ann-Marie after reminding them of the beginning of the Micmac tale, "the boy knew that the old couple couldn't afford to feed him. They had barely enough for themselves. In fact the whole Micmac village was poor and the people hungry as slaves, so the boy decided to become a hunter. He hunted on land, he hunted at sea, but no one had taught him, and he didn't have much luck."

"He needed to be learnt things, like we are," interrupted Corey. Rachel beamed at him with surprise and pride.

"Just so," Ann-Marie went on. "But with the help of the old man, he made himself a bow and arrow and a harpoon. He practised and practised and practised on old stumps of trees and bushes and such. One day, thinking that perhaps he'd practised enough, he saw a great whale in the sea and caught it all by himself. He dragged it onto the beach and ran to fetch the old couple. Then the old lady took a knife and cut the whale up, making sure to throw its bones back into the ocean so it would grow again. Now there was plenty of food for the boy, the old couple, and the whole village, right through the winter."

"Wish we could catch a whale," Molasses said sadly. She looked hungry and pinched, and her face was quite dry and smooth, like there wasn't any more treacle in her house.

They all sighed. Quickly Rachel picked up a stick and began to draw letters in the soil and first flakes of snow. D E F. "They're the second lot of letters in the alphabet. This is the noise they make." She sounded them out. "What did I teach you last time?"

"A B C," called out a little boy in the back.

"Well done," came a deep growly voice. Rachel jumped. It was Colonel Blucke, fresh out of his fancy house down the shore. He was wearing his long coat, a cocked hat, and carrying a cane.

"Rachel? You Titan's girl?"

"Yessuh." She sounded like Hannah, but Colonel Blucke was a big important person in Birchtown. Even if you didn't know that, even if no one had ever told you, you'd work it out just by looking at him. Rachel could glimpse his shiny breeches buckles glinting out from under his coat, and the trace of a clean shirt ruffle around his neck. Colonel Blucke was rich as most white folk. You *could* say he was the mayor of Birchtown. And you wouldn't be far wrong.

"You're doing a fine job with these Negro children. Come and speak to me tomorrow afternoon."

"Yessuh, I will."

"When the sun reaches just past its highest point."

Rachel nodded.

And just like that, Colonel Blucke was gone along the path towards Shelburne, leaving Rachel quaking in the shoes that Missus Pritchard had given her. What on earth could someone as big and important as Colonel Blucke want with a little nobody of a Nigra like her?

There was a scratching at the door. Titan was out cutting wood, and Hannah had taken Jem down to where the sea met the pond to fill a pail with the blood-coloured water. Rachel was all by herself.

"Miz Rachel? You there? It's me, Molasses."

Rachel ran to let her in.

"I had to come. It was the story that Micmac girl told. We ain't got no food, Miz Rachel, not one scrap. Our supplies all run out, and those of the next-door folk too. There's six of us children all in that little pit hole with nothin' to eat. We gonna starve this winter, sure an' certain."

Rachel thought of the whale. She thought of how it fed the whole Micmac village and how its bones got thrown back into the sea to make more whale. She thought of the four golden guineas in her chink in the wall. Titan was bringing in a little money still. He was a skilled carpenter. They would manage somehow.

"Turn your back," she told Molasses sharply. Two minutes later, after a mighty shiver of worry and hesitation, Rachel gave Molasses a broad piece, shutting it tight into the other girl's hand before she changed her mind.

"What's this?" The girl, alarmed, peeked through the gaps in her fingers at the glint of gold that lay in her palm. She'd never seen anything half so brilliant or shiny before.

"It'll get you through the winter. Give it to your daddy. He'll know what to do with it."

"Yessum."

"And don't you go letting anybody know about it outside your family."

"No'um."

After Molasses left, grinning and crying, Rachel returned to her hidey-hole and counted the guineas. Now there were three. She had just wanted to make sure.

CHAPTER N.º 5

"*Well,*" *said the colonel as he folded one*
leg over the other and leaned back in his seat. "You
surely are doing a good job with those Negro
children hereabouts. I've been thinking of starting
a school myself. Who taught you how to read?"

Rachel was drinking tea out of a pretty blue-
and-white cup in Colonel Blucke's big house,
trying not to choke. He had real furniture, and
rugs, and shutters on the windows. Pretty glasses
and patterned dishes were lined up on the
shelves. The tea had streamed out of a big china
teapot, and there were even slop and sugar bowls

on the tray that sat on the table. It was difficult not to get distracted by the richness of the place.

She sat ramrod straight in her chair and concentrated real hard. "Nathan Crowley, a white boy, suh, and Missus Pritchard." She figured this needed some explaining, and she was worried as well about telling him that a white boy had taught her the alphabet. So she added a little more, first a sentence, then a sip of tea, then another sentence, then another sip, until the whole story was out in the open and the tea was nothing but dregs. She wouldn't have left that tea undrunk for anything. It had real cubes of sugar in it. And Mamma had once said that a tea leaf was just like a little shimmer of gold dust, worth about as much, too.

"A white boy?" asked the colonel, his eyebrows knitting together.

"Yessuh. I met him in the woods once, and he's been awful kind."

"Well, good for him and good for you. Teaching and learning, you could say, are as valuable as a drawer full of guineas."

Rachel swallowed hard, though there wasn't a jot of tea left, neither in her mouth nor in the cup.

"Anyway," said the colonel, changing the subject, "you can't go on teaching those little ones out there much longer. It's growing far too cold."

"Yessuh, you're right. I've been a heap worried over that. If we leave their learning till spring, they'll have forgotten mostly everything they know. Besides, it's hard enough to get the knowledge into their heads in the first place without most of it falling out again." Rachel was concerned that maybe she'd said too much, but felt she had to go on. "I'd teach them over the winter, but our house is much too small for all of them."

Colonel Blucke grinned a big wide friendly grin, and his eyes crinkled. "I've got a fine big house, with only me, my wife, and our servant knocking around in it. There's a large front entrance with no furniture of any value in it. You'll have seen it on your way in. You could teach those Negroes there."

"I could?"

"Yes, missy, and then maybe come the spring we'll build a real schoolhouse, like the white folk have over in Shelburne. I'll even throw in a bit of the teaching of the arithmetic myself. The Negro children need learning, same as everyone else."

"Now isn't that what I'm always saying? I'm sure they're just as clever deep down. You can't tell the depth of a well by the length of the pump-handle." A sudden tear dropped into her cup. She had sounded just like Mamma.

"Why, what is it, child?"

Rachel wavered for a moment. She really didn't know how much Colonel Blucke would want to hear, big important person that he was. But then she decided to go right ahead anyhow—what was the harm?—and tell him about picking *bluebetties,* and Serjeant and George Gyssop, and how Mamma had been taken back a slave. She had vanished just as surely as snow melted into spring streams.

"I know about that already. Just about everyone all the way to Shelburne knows it." The colonel looked grim, his wide smile suddenly shrunk to a narrow slash across his face, and for a moment Rachel felt she'd done wrong to bring the matter up in the first place. But the colonel soon turned back to the business of learning.

"You'll need to go from hut to hut and from one pit-cabin to the next to let the children know they'll be taught here. You teach *them,* and when I've time for it, I'll teach *you,* further your education a little. Now, how would that be?"

"That would be very fine, suh. And my Micmac friend, Ann-Marie?"

"She's welcome too. I think she's entitled to a bit of learning." He had said nothing about Mamma, so Rachel reckoned she shouldn't say anything more either. Instead she murmured her goodbyes and stammered out her thanks. Two minutes later she was on her way to fetch Hannah, who was cleaning out the grate in the fireplace. She quickly told her what was what. Then the two of them, swinging Jem between them, rushed from house to house and one pit-cabin to another in the early snow, telling all the Nigra children that there'd be school the next morning and every day till Christmas, excepting church days. And there was much clapping of hands and dancing up and down, and many a broad grin on a thin face. Though Hannah was quick to say afterwards that all this learning taxed a Nigra's brains something awful and she couldn't see, all things taken into account, why it was held to be such a good idea.

CHAPTER N.º 6

It had been a horrible morning. All Rachel had ever really wanted was to learn to read and write, and work out how to teach other Nigras, so they'd all have a chance, but now she saw that the second part of her dream, teaching the Nigra children, was going to be much harder than she'd reckoned on. She hadn't the training for it, perhaps not the talent either. About thirty-five had turned up, eager to learn, or see what was what, or just cause trouble—maybe because it was too cold to play outside. Worst of all, Ann-Marie was nowhere to be found, perhaps too shy to come into the fancy place.

At first mostly all the children except a few bold boys were awed by the Blucke house and couldn't even stammer out so much as a word, not even an A or a B or a C, though somehow Corey had miraculously changed from the worst little nuisance into her star pupil. But quicker than it took to drink a cup of water, nearly all the children got rowdy as de-listed soldiers. Two boys pulled Molasses' hair till she cried, one boy punched another because his legs were in the way, two small girls pushed a third away from them, saying she smelled like a skunk, and Jem escaped Hannah, crawling into another room and smashing an expensive dish that belonged to the Bluckes. The noise quieted them all, but only for a second.

"See, I told you so," Hannah's eyes seemed to say, as if it wasn't her fault but Rachel's. Rachel thought maybe Hannah had let go of the baby on purpose because she didn't want to put up with all this "learnin' nonsense," as she put it, and besides, she looked about as innocent as a cat who'd just swallowed a mouse, tail and all. Rachel wanted to shake her hard, knock some sense or alphabet into her. Only Corey, quite amazingly, had been good, sitting on the floor with his face scrubbed and his hair slicked down like a proper little gentleman, patiently waiting to talk about the joys of being clean as havoc roared around him. Today he really *was* her star pupil.

Colonel Blucke poked his head around the door twice, both times when the racket was so bad it came back and punched Rachel in the face. She wanted to do something silly and violent, slap one of the children maybe, like the old slave missus on the plantation had slapped her. Instead, when she saw the colonel's face the second time, she bent down and pulled on her bootlaces so tight they snapped. It stopped her from doing something dreadful. Still, he would turn them out for sure now that he saw how wicked and unheeding the children were, how impossible it was for her to control them. But,

"You need to keep those Negroes busy," was all he said, mildly. "Don't let them rule the roost. I'll see if I can find some primers or hornbooks for them in Shelburne. It's the weather too. Bad weather makes for bad children."

As soon as class was over, Rachel parted company with Hannah and Jem and made for the woods. Frost slicked the path. It was freezing as February, and snow was blowing in vast fluffy clouds off the sea. But she had to be on her own for at least the length of a mockingbird's song. She just had to, or she'd never sort out her mind. Not that there were any mockingbirds around here. Why were the children so bad? Why couldn't they be more grateful? And who was she to think she could ever, ever teach them anything? "All this time you been thinking you Miss High and Mighty," she grumbled to herself, almost in Hannah's voice, "but truth to tell, you just the same as any other poor Nigra."

She was so busy scolding herself she barely noticed another girl standing in front of her.

"As if I haven't seen enough Nigra children for one day," she groaned. But then she stared in dismay. The child, although smaller and clearly younger than she was, seemed almost her mirror image, straight and tall with dark skin and tightly braided hair. Rachel could have sworn she was looking at herself, or at least, herself as she'd been three or four years back. She knew she should say something, but didn't know what.

"Hello," said the little girl. "I seed you coming out that big house. I been watching you."

She was dreadfully, painfully thin, Rachel realized, now that she was looking at the girl properly. One good gust would likely blow her away. "I haven't seen you before. What's your name?"

"Rachel," the girl replied promptly, and the bigger Rachel almost fainted.

"Why, that's my name too. I never did hear of any other Nigra having that name before. Where's your mamma and your daddy?"

"Further along in the woods." The girl jerked her head sideways as if to indicate where they might be found. "We just come to Birchtown. We was slaves before, but the massa threw us out."

"You from Shelburne?"

"No. Way, way east, my daddy says. We been walking long days."

And now that Rachel had gotten over her shock and come to think on it, the child did look tired as a dog that wouldn't leave off chasing its tail. But it was really none of Rachel's business. She couldn't be dealing with now-and-then folk, the passersby who came and went in Birchtown between one sneeze and another. She had enough problems of her own. She spun around and began running down the hill towards home.

"My mamma's awful sick," the girl cried after her. She didn't add, "Can you help any?" but Rachel knew only too well what she meant. And if there was one thing guaranteed to bring Rachel back, it was someone else's mamma being sick. Her own mamma had been sick too when they first came to Birchtown, sick almost to death, and Rachel had gone mad with worry. It had taken Ann-Marie's aunt with her Micmac ways and medicine bag to heal her. Rachel owed for that, she owed big. And sometimes you paid those kinds of debts by helping out someone else in the same kind of trouble. She sighed and turned slowly to face the girl.

"What's wrong with her?"

"Too much walking, no food. She's just bone-tired, can't get up."

"You'd better take me to see her," Rachel said. Her sigh was almost big enough to blow all the snow clouds out of the sky.

Little Rachel's mamma was lying flat out on a rock, her breath going into her with a sharp huff and coming back out again with a sharp puff. "Need some food," she whispered. Her eyes were

closed and her eyelids had a bluish tinge to them. But it was at the little girl's daddy that Rachel stared most. He seemed tall as a mountain, even taller than Titan. He was dark and his limbs were straight and he looked familiar. It was as if Rachel had seen him before, perhaps in a dream.

"What be your name?" the man asked suddenly, drawing himself up higher than a pine tree. Rachel jumped.

"Rachel, suh," she said. He was the kind of person you just couldn't help saying "suh" to.

"And where you be from?"

"Down the hill in Birchtown, suh."

"No, I mean where you be from *before*."

"From New York, and before that, Charlestown, in South Carolina."

"What be your mamma's name?"

"Sukey, suh. Sukey Sparrow."

"I don't know about no Sparrow," said the man, "but I did know a Sukey once, long time ago, down in the South where they bring in the rice. I know'd her real well. She spoke those

African sayings real grand. And she had a little baby named Rachel, just like I call my young daughter here." The man's dark brown eyes went all blurry like he was crying.

And suddenly Rachel Sparrow understood. She didn't even have to figure it out. She had come face to face with her daddy. Her *real* daddy, not a stepdaddy like Titan. The daddy who'd been sold away from the plantation when she was very tiny. The daddy who was the reason she was so dark and straight and tall. He must have called his second daughter Rachel as a remembrance of her. By accident he'd found his way back to his first daughter. And Rachel could tell he knew that as well as she did.

"You come on down the hill with me," she said. "I'll give you what you need to buy as much food as you can eat. To make your wife a heap better and fatten up your daughter. And maybe you could even build a hut right here in Birchtown." She was thinking very hard. "You could stay near us in the meantime. There's a pit-cabin we used to live in that will do for a time. Mamma lives with Titan, my stepdaddy. She's gone for a while. But she'll be so pleased to see you when she gets back."

Rachel stopped, out of breath. She couldn't waste her brain space trying to figure out how to tell Titan that her real daddy was here. Or wondering what might happen when Mamma came back. *If* Mamma came back. Those were puzzles for the future. But she knew what she had to do right now. Little Rachel's mamma was starving, so there wasn't too much time. She would give two of the three remaining guineas to the little family, her mirror family. There were three of them after all, their plight was worse than anyone else's, and when everything was said and done the big tall man was her very own daddy. Afterwards she would have one guinea left. She didn't need Colonel Blucke to teach her more of the arithmetic to know that. Only one shining golden guinea would remain all by itself in her treasure trove, her little hidey-hole back at the house. But it would be all right. It would have to be. She, Titan, Jem, and even Hannah would manage to get through the winter because every now and then Nathan Crowley, true to his word, was bringing them all kinds of cheap fill-the-belly food from that bad-smell-under-the-nose store-keeper in Shelburne. They would all get by somehow, new family and old. But she sighed. She was ready to laugh and cry at the same time. Her daddy, her real true daddy, was here. She'd never thought to see him again. But thanks to bumping into little Rachel on the hill, now she had a new father and a new sister and a kind-of-starving stepmother. In fact, she had an enormous heap of people to worry her mind about.

Her family was growing and growing, spreading out branches, which put down roots, which grew into new trunks. She was recollecting one of those enormous banyan trees in Africa that Mamma had once told her about. Banyan trees, grey and many-footed, Mamma had said, were the trapped spirits of elephants. If you waited long enough, most likely when the moon was round and bright as one of Rachel's golden guineas and the night was young as Jem, you might surely see one of those trees pick up its roots and boughs and go tromping through the jungle.

An elephant tree, decided Rachel, who had seen neither a banyan nor an elephant in her entire life. Her family was an elephant tree. But she now had two daddies and had to figure out where each of them belonged in her scheme of things.

"Yes," said her new true daddy, interrupting her thoughts. "I come down the hill with you."

CHAPTER №7

It was near Christmas. Ann-Marie had at last crept into classes at the big Blucke house.

"I didn't tell the whole story to the children," she whispered to Rachel. "Do you think I should?"

"What's left to tell?"

"That the old woman died, leaving the old man and the boy together."

"I think we might leave that part out," said Rachel. "There's been too much want and death for most of these Nigras already. Perhaps you could start on another story after I've taught them their M N O." But as she taught the unruly class their letters she came round to thinking scary thoughts about the story. The boy had caught the whale just as she had "caught" the golden guineas from the Pritchards. Then, in the Micmac tale, pieces of the whale had been given out to stop the village starving. She was doing the same kind of thing. She had given a guinea to Nathan Crowley to use for her family because Hannah was an extra mouth to feed. She had given a guinea to Molasses, whose face was all sticky again because there was treacle in her pit-cabin once more. And she had given two guineas to her new father so that his wife would recover and little Rachel would grow fat. She had sworn everyone to secrecy of course.

The old woman, a kind of mother to the boy in the story, had died when all the pieces of cut-up whale had been given out. Did that mean that Mamma was dead too, or at least that she would sure as sugar die if Rachel was stupid enough to give the last glittering guinea away? She shuddered, decided to keep that last guinea till the end of creation, no matter how hard up some folk in Birchtown might be, no matter how sad their tales of woe. It might be an imagining or it might really be a heap of bad luck to bestow it. She would keep it safe in the hidey-hole back at her house.

Colonel Blucke poked his head around the door, looking mighty serious. "I'm going away for a few days. I'm just about to saddle my horse and be gone. But you can keep on teaching right till Christmas Eve. My wife is here if you need anything." Then he poked his head back like a turtle going into its shell.

That meant no more of the arithmetic lessons for a while, but Rachel didn't really mind that. Although Colonel Blucke was a kind man, she didn't really like arithmetic, couldn't get the hang of subtracting or adding numbers above ten. She sure could count those guineas, though, that she had given away. She went through them yet again in her head.

She ended class early. As the Nigra children dispersed noisily, she began to walk along the shore to her home. A pile of untidy problems were growing into a mountain of trouble in her head. The students still made a racket louder than heaven's trumpet most of the time and would behave even worse with the colonel gone. One good glare of his usually simmered them down, but Rachel didn't have that kind of glare. On top of that she still hadn't told Titan about her new daddy and his family, who now lived in the Sparrows' old pit-cabin. And she still fretted like crazy about Mamma. She was worrying so hard she didn't even notice when little Corey, clean and neat, started to walk beside her.

"Miz Rachel?"

"Yes, Corey?"

"I sad."

"Why is that, Corey?"

"Can't tell you, Miz Rachel, not no-how. Nanna Jacklin told me not to tell no one."

"Oh dear," Rachel said. "I think you'd better tell me, Corey. You can't just say you're sad and then refuse to tell me why." From the look on Corey's gleaming scrubbed face she had a feeling she was about to hear very bad news indeed.

Corey hesitated.

"Go on, Corey. I really need to know."

"Nanna Jacklin will skin me if I tell."

"I'll skin you if you don't."

Corey gave a big sigh. "Well, Miz Rachel, there are no bebbies bein' born—at least not to rich ol' fambilies—and so Nanna Jacklin ain't bein' paid nothin'."

"Oh dear," Rachel said again.

"So we is hungry as a bear after winter, Miz Rachel. Only the water in the streams is free, and that's why I always looks so nice and clean, jus' like you told me to be."

Oh dear, oh dear, oh dear, Rachel thought, kicking a stone out of her way. *Mamma,* her heart screamed. *Corey and Nanna Jacklin,* her brain shouted. Somewhere along the line, without her even noticing, Corey and Nanna had become part of her family, the ears, perhaps, of her elephant tree. It was as if Mamma was on one side of an argument and Nanna Jacklin and Corey were on the other, as if they were being weighed against each other on the scales that the stuck-up storekeeper kept in her shop. For a moment Rachel couldn't make up her mind. What should she do? Mamma, if she was alive, was far away. There was no way Rachel could help her. Nanna Jacklin and Corey, on the other hand, were here, and they were starving. She could certainly change that. The scales tipped in their favour with a sad clang.

"You'd better come along with me," she said to Corey at last. "I have something that will help, but you're not to tell a soul in the whole wide world. Nanna Jacklin won't be cross with you, I promise, but she's not to tell a soul neither."

"Never, Miz Rachel. I'll makes sure she knows."

"Make," Rachel corrected him. "You'll *make* sure ..."

"Yessum," he replied solemnly. "I'll *make* sure she *know*."

Now not one guinea would remain. And it wasn't like throwing whale bones back in the water. No new guineas would grow. Suppose, in a mysterious kind of way, it affected Mamma? Suppose Mamma died? Rachel's heart dropped down to her toes. But more was to follow. The very next day.

"*New folk living in our old pit-cabin,*" said Titan, breaking his usual silence.

"Yes, Titan." Rachel's pulse was fluttering in her throat, but she tried to sound like nothing was wrong. "They've been there awhile." Oh, why hadn't she told Titan the truth when she had the chance? She bit her lip.

Her stepdaddy was already out of his seat by the fireplace, slipping his long thin feet into his long thin shoes, and it didn't take too much imagining to guess he was on his way down there. Was he going to chuck them out into the snow? She couldn't bear to think of it.

"It's really cold," she ventured timidly, but he had that hard set look on his face that she had seen before. There was nothing for it but to go with him. Rachel tied her bootlaces, flung on her coat, and followed him. The snow was really deep now, creeping cold and wet inside the top of her boots.

With Titan's long stride and Rachel half running to keep up with him, it took much less time than she would have liked to reach the old cabin.

"Titan?"

"Um?"

And then Rachel told him. She told him her real true daddy lived in there. She told him about how sick his wife had been. She told him about her new sister. And then, just for good measure, as Mamma would say, she threw in the truth about the five golden guineas and how she'd given them all away, just like the boy in Ann-Marie's Micmac story had shared his pieces of whale with the whole village. Everything came out in a sorry rush.

"Five guineas?" Titan repeated, his eyes like stones. He must be working up to be very, very mad at her.

"Yes, Titan. I'm mighty sorry."

"Those people must have needed it more than we," was all he said. And he kept walking.

Now the trap door in the pit-cabin roof was just visible, and he knocked on it. Rachel remembered those miserable days in that old pit-cabin. She hoped the rest of her elephant tree family weren't doing too badly.

In a trice the trap door opened, and the head and shoulders of Rachel's daddy appeared. He was so tall that even with his feet planted on the pit-cabin floor, he still stood eye to eye with his daughter.

"Hello," he said, looking upwards from Rachel to Titan.

"Hello," replied Titan. "This was our cabin."

"Yes, I know."

Silence. Rachel was scared.

"Pretty uncomfortable. In spring, when the land comes unfrozen, I'll help you build a hut," Titan said fast and clipped, like he'd just made up his mind.

"Thank you," said Rachel's daddy. "This be fine for us now. Your Rachel, she was kind enough to offer it, but my wife and daughter need good shelter, so that be mighty kind of you."

"I have a wife too, when she comes back. Name of Sukey."

"I know that too," said Rachel's daddy.

"So I reckon we're both suited."

"I reckon that be true."

The two men shook hands, and Titan sloped back through the forest in his flimsy shoes, with Rachel slipping and sliding behind him. Why, she reckoned he'd known all the time who the little family was. He must have seen her daddy before, tall and dark and straight-limbed like the man's older daughter. Or maybe he'd spied her little sister, Rachel, who was the dead spit of her. Titan had put two and two together, just like with the colonel's arithmetic. Titan was such a clever man. Rachel wondered now whether she'd needed to tell him anything. Except maybe about the guineas. She wondered too if her confession had changed his course. Maybe he would have thrown her other family out if she hadn't owned up to knowing them. She shivered all the way home.

CHAPTER N° 9

It was Christmas Eve. Rachel had taught her last class of the year and the children had behaved like a pack of wild dogs. Even little Rachel, who had just joined the others, was giggling and shifting around like she had ants under her backside. Colonel Blucke still hadn't returned and the children thought that gave them a certificate of freedom. Not the slave kind. The school kind. It wasn't that they were excited about Christmas, for in most cases nothing special was promising to come their way. It was that they were mighty pleased to be getting a week off from "the book learnin'," as they now all termed it, courtesy of Hannah. She still managed to say "book learnin'" or "learnin' nonsense," with her nose stuck straight up in the air, as if it were a deathly disease. And since they'd all found out school was a deal harder than they'd expected it to be, they mostly agreed with her.

Still, now they knew their letters all the way to their Y and their Z, which Rachel had taught them this morning. As long as none of the early letters had dropped out of their brains. That was the problem, she sometimes thought. When you pushed one bit of knowledge in, another flew out. You couldn't keep it all in there together unless you maybe locked their heads with a big brass key.

"The Y is like two boughs dividing on a great oak tree. The Z is a big old zag of lightning," she told them, hoping that if they saw those letters as pictures, they would stick. But her voice was a whisper in the din.

"Shut your silly Nigra mouths!" she had yelled suddenly. And they were so shocked they all did, at least for a moment. Then they went back to messing and giggling.

She had almost wept with weariness. "I don't know what to do with these Nigras," she told Ann-Marie, "and with the colonel away I'm not getting any lessons myself." Ann-Marie clucked sympathetically, but said nothing.

Rachel was glad to make her way home with Hannah and Jem. It was a relief to be inside, away from the snow and the naughty children. But even the hut was miserable. The pale tongues of fire licked the smoky lips of the fireplace, but not a shimmer of warmth reached beyond the grate. There was little for dinner, just scant bowls of cornmeal. Nathan Crowley seemed to have forgotten the Sparrows. He hadn't brought any belly-filling food for weeks, nor any other kind neither, no doubt too taken up with Christmas in *his* house to worry about Christmas in theirs. Jem cried and cried, pulling at his gums. Titan sat in a corner, head drooping.

Oh dear. No matter how many people there were in the little hut, it was still dreary as a foggy day. That was because Mamma wasn't there. She'd never come home now. Rachel should have kept that last guinea. It had been a heap of bad luck to give it away. If nothing else, she could have spent it on Christmas. Now they had nothing to look forward to.

Snow was falling through the chimney. The fire sputtered and died. Rachel felt as wretched as she'd ever felt in her whole life, worse even than when she was a slave back in South Carolina.

Suddenly there was a knock at the door. Who could it be, out in this terrible weather? Rachel rushed to open it, hoping against hope to see Mamma. It wasn't Mamma, of course. She was too long gone to turn up on the doorstep like a three-penny piece that had rolled around the table and come back to its owner. But Ann-Marie was standing there with all Rachel's students, Corey and little Rachel among them. They were smiling, didn't seem in the least to mind the snow falling between their necks and collars.

"These children want to tell you something," said Ann-Marie.

Molasses stepped forward. "Please, Miz Rachel, we just want to say we sorry for bein' so bad. Book learnin' is good. Bein' clever Nigras is even better. We can't wait to start school again. Leastways it warm in Massa Blucke's house. And I brought you a special something for bein' so kind to me and mine." Molasses held out a tiny bowl of treacle.

A moment later Nanna Jacklin joined them. "Merry Christmas," she said, holding out a cup of *blackbetty* jam. Rachel took the treacle in one hand, the jam in the other.

"Thank you all very much," she beamed. "It will be a sweet Christmas."

She took the gifts into the house and came straight back. Titan, curious, and Hannah, carrying Jem, came back with her. Other Nigras were beginning to gather, coming to see what all the fuss was about. Among them were Rachel's real true daddy and his wife, who was looking a deal more healthy.

"I brung you this," her daddy said to her, holding out a tiny doll whittled from wood. "I been carrying it about all these years. It wasn't yours, but I fashioned it to be a reminder of you. You be the reason I called my new daughter Rachel. I be pleasantly hoping she grow up like you."

There was a tiny rustle. Glancing sideways, Rachel could see Nathan Crowley hiding behind a tall fir a ways off. She could tell him by his silver-buckled shoes, half buried by snow. They stuck out from the bottom of the tree like roots. He wouldn't reveal himself with all these Nigras around. She'd get to speak to him later though. And she knew he'd have a mound of food for them. How could she have imagined, even for one minute, that he would forget her? Now Rachel was crying. She hadn't realized that so many people cared about her.

"Make way, make way," came a deep growly voice. It was Colonel Blucke, returned at last, just in time for Christmas. The folk of Birchtown separated into two cornrows, waiting for him to pass through. Then Rachel saw. The colonel wasn't riding his great brown horse. He was leading it. Sitting atop the animal, looking more than a mite uncomfortable, was Mamma!

"They beasts sure do make you backside stiff," she complained, sliding off the horse and into the snow with a bump. Rachel and Titan ran to hug her.

After a minute the colonel approached them, speaking so only they could hear. "I traced Miz Sparrow down with the help of the white men's records," he said. "George Gyssop had moved to Halifax. And there's one more thing ..." He seemed to be addressing Rachel.

"Yessuh?" she replied.

"I've spoken to the white folk over in Shelburne. They're going to give us money for a school, Rachel Sparrow, a real school. We'll build it soon as the earth warms in spring. I'm to be schoolmaster, but you'll be my assistant. I'll be paying you a shilling a week to get all that learning into those Negro heads."

Rachel gasped. Mamma back. And a whole shilling. And a proper teaching place. She didn't know what to say. So she bobbed a curtsey instead. Colonel Blucke smiled a big friendly smile. It was kind of lopsided, truth to tell, like he wasn't used to creasing his face lately. He led his horse away. The crowd began to disperse.

"Come back later," Rachel whispered to Ann-Marie.

"I'll try. Merry Christmas." Ann-Marie disappeared into the woods, and the Sparrows went indoors. Rachel put her new doll down on the table.

"You never guess what happen," said Mamma. "Colonel Blucke, he talk gruff to that old George

Gyssop, he give him what for and tell him to pay me." Her fingers opened like dark rose petals unfurling. Five golden guineas glinted in her palm. "Bet you never see such money in your whole life, girl," she grinned at Rachel.

"Yes, Mamma. No, Mamma." Rachel smiled a secret smile. "And we got surprises for you too. Just you wait and see." She hugged Mamma again. She thought she'd never get through with hugging her.

At that moment there came a second knock at the door. That would be Nathan, with all their Christmas food. Before letting him in, Rachel looked around. At Mamma, at Titan, at Jem, and at Hannah, who seemed to fit in for good and all. Now that Nathan had turned up, there were just a few more people to come. Rachel's daddy, his wife, and her new little sister. Maybe Ann-Marie too. And Corey and Nanna Jacklin. Then, though times were still mean, for sure there would be frolics tonight: singing and dancing, eating and drinking, jumping up and down with the sheer joy of living. That was the way of it, sure enough. For Rachel. And for her entire elephant tree family.

ACKNOWLEDGEMENTS

Many thanks to my dear husband, Michael; to my family and friends, who have stuck by me through good times and bad; to Corey Guy, and to Clara and Ernestine of the Jacklyn family, all descendants of the Black Loyalists; to Laird Niven, the archaeologist of the Birchtown Site; to Patricia Clark of Seneca College; to Ron Lightburn, who drew the enchanting illustrations that accompany the text; to Leona Trainer, my dear friend and former agent who encouraged me to send in my work; to Barbara Berson, my original editor, and Cindy Kantor, who brought the idea for the series to Penguin; to Jennifer Notman, who is working on the treasury edition; to all those at Penguin who have had a role in publishing *Rachel*; to all those who were kind enough to list the original Rachel books for awards; to all the young people who read them and wrote to me about them; to the dedicated doctors, nurses, and volunteers at the University Health Network; and to Willow and Merlin, shelties extraordinaire, who keep me on my toes and will do almost anything for a cookie.

1608
Samuel de Champlain establishes the first fortified trading post at Quebec.

1759
The British defeat the French in the Battle of the Plains of Abraham.

1812
The United States declares war against Canada.

1845
The expedition of Sir John Franklin to the Arctic ends when the ship is frozen in the pack ice; the fate of its crew remains a mystery.

1869
Louis Riel leads his Métis followers in the Red River Rebellion.

1871
British Columbia joins Canada.

1755
The British expel the entire French population of Acadia (today's Maritime provinces), sending them into exile.

1776
The 13 Colonies revolt against Britain, and the Loyalists flee to Canada.

1837
Calling for responsible government, the Patriotes, following Louis-Joseph Papineau, rebel in Lower Canada; William Lyon Mackenzie leads the uprising in Upper Canada.

1867
New Brunswick, Nova Scotia and the United Province of Canada come together in Confederation to form the Dominion of Canada.

1870
Manitoba joins Canada. The Northwest Territories become an official territory of Canada.

1783
Rachel

Timeline

1885
At Craigellachie, British Columbia, the last spike is driven to complete the building of the Canadian Pacific Railway.

1898
The Yukon Territory becomes an official territory of Canada.

1914
Britain declares war on Germany, and Canada, because of its ties to Britain, is at war too.

1918
As a result of the Wartime Elections Act, the women of Canada are given the right to vote in federal elections.

1945
World War II ends conclusively with the dropping of atomic bombs on Hiroshima and Nagasaki.

1873
Prince Edward Island joins Canada.

1896
Gold is discovered on Bonanza Creek, a tributary of the Klondike River.

1905
Alberta and Saskatchewan join Canada.

1917
In the Halifax harbour, two ships collide, causing an explosion that leaves more than 1,600 dead and 9,000 injured.

1939
Canada declares war on Germany seven days after war is declared by Britain and France.

1949
Newfoundland, under the leadership of Joey Smallwood, joins Canada.

1896
Emily

1885
Marie-Claire

1917
Penelope

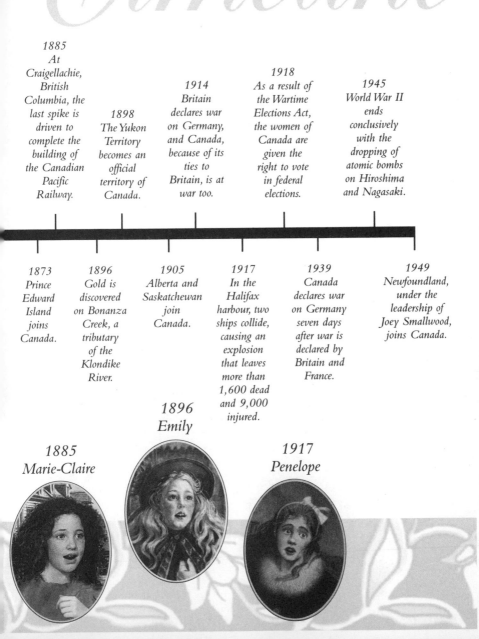